THE
SORCERER'S
APPRENTICE

FRANÇOIS AUGIÉRAS

THE SORCERER'S APPRENTICE

Translated from the French by
Sue Dyson

PUSHKIN PRESS
LONDON

For BrP

First published in *Cahier des Saisons*, Éditions Julliard in 1964

Translation copyright © Sue Dyson 2001

This edition first published in 2001 by
Pushkin Press
82 Selkirk Road
London SW17 0EP

British Library Cataloguing in Publication Data:
A catalogue record for this book is available
from the British Library

ISBN 1 901285 44 8

Frontispiece: Roger-Viollet, Paris

Set in 10.5 on 13.5 Baskerville
and printed in Britain
by Sherlock Printing, Bolney, West Sussex
on Legend Laid paper

THE
SORCERER'S
APPRENTICE

IN PÉRIGORD there lived a priest. His house stood high above a village made up of twenty dilapidated dwellings with grey stone roofs. These houses straggled up the side of the hill, to meet old, bramble-filled gardens, the church and the adjoining presbytery, which were built on rocks reflected in the River Vézère, flowing past at their base. Few people lived there; this priest served several parishes, which meant that, since he spent all day travelling round the countryside, he did not return home until evening. He was aged around thirty-five, just about as unpleasant as a priest can be, and although this was all my parents knew about him, they had entrusted me to his care, urging him to deal strictly with me. Which indeed he did, as you will see.

On the evening of my arrival, the sky was a soft shade of gold. He did not offer me any supper; the moment I turned up on his doorstep he took me straight to my room, which was located in a corridor as ugly as himself. Leaving the door ajar, he abandoned me without a word, if you discount a few unanswerable phrases, such as: every cloud has a silver lining; the tables are turned; come what may; sleep well in the arms of Morpheus; and other such drivel. I

9

heard him go into the next bedroom, moving about, doing God knows what, talking to himself, then there was silence.

I had been asleep for less than an hour when I was awakened by a terrible howling. Sitting bolt upright in bed, my eyes wide open, I waited for what seemed an eternity, petrified that I would hear another sound as terrible as the first. But nothing else disturbed the silence of the night. The moon picked out a few leafy branches among the shadows in a wild garden behind the presbytery; its beautiful rays shone through the panes of my little window, lighting up the corner of a table covered with my blue school notebooks, and a whitewashed wall, and faintly outlining the rim of a water-jug. I was sleepy; I drifted off again without worrying too much about my extravagant priest's odd ways, for it was he who had shouted out in the next room, which was separated from mine only by a thin partition wall.

In the morning, when I went downstairs, I found my parish priest in an almost good mood, making coffee. I owe it to him to mention that at his house I drank the best coffee in the world, delicate yet strong, with a curious taste of embers and ash. He took a great deal of care preparing it according to his own method, all the time muttering away, not to me, but to the flames which he blew on gently, rekindling the embers, talking

THE SORCERER'S APPRENTICE

to them as if they were people. He removed the coffee
from the heat as soon as it began to bubble, returning
it for a brief instant to the burning coals which he
picked up in his bare fingers, as though he derived
enjoyment from the act, and without noticeably burning himself. The whole process took a good quarter of
an hour, and he spent the entire time crouched in the
hearth, with his cassock bunched up between his thighs.

After we had drunk our coffee, we went out into the
garden. Sitting on some steps, at the intersection of
two pathways, he got me to translate some Latin passage or other from my school books. As far as I could
see, he had a rather poor grasp of Latin. He had the
unpleasant habit of vigorously scratching his horrible
black hair, and that got on my nerves. What's more,
he kept reminding me how grateful I should be to my
parents, who had had the excellent idea of entrusting me
to him. If my attention wandered, even for a moment,
he seized me by the ear and I felt two hard, sharp fin-
gernails sink into my flesh. He wore a disgustingly dirty
cassock, for he was extremely mean with money, and
thought he looked good in it. He addressed me by the
sweetest names, while at the same time poking fun at
me; he displayed the polite manner one might use
when celebrating a small Mass; he kept calling me
"Young Sir"; it was as if he were saying: I'm only a
peasant, I owe you a little politeness; and there you

have it, all in one go; try to be content with it, young Gentleman. This Latin lesson, punctuated with little courtesies, lasted no more than a page; he stood up; I did likewise, and both of us were delighted that it was over—in my case the Latin, in his, the politeness. To tell the truth, in that June of my sixteenth year, what I really wanted were language lessons of a different kind, for love is a language, even more ancient than Latin (and there are those who say even that defies decency).

Leaving me to Seneca and Caesar, he strode off into the countryside. He had charge of several parishes; very well then, let him leave me on my own, this solitude would not be without its attractions; I was perfectly capable of passing the time and getting by without my priest.

As soon as he had gone, I put down my books and gave up trying to follow Caesar's conquests; instead, I opened my eyes wide and took a long look at my new life. All along the banks of the Vézère ran the vast, thickly-wooded hills of the Sarladais. Closer to me, our garden was broken up by little low walls made of heaped-up stones, and by steps and pathways. All kinds of plants were jumbled up together, growing wild, almost hiding the once-ordered layout of a rather fine formal garden. Everything flourished higgledy-piggledy, rose bushes and brambles, flowers, grass and fruit trees. This lost order reinforced the garden's charm, as well as the anxiety which you felt as you tried to find your way round that tangled mess, whose traceries of flowers were bizarrely watched over by a pale blue plaster statue of the Virgin Mary. She rose above the wild jumble of plants, looking just a touch simple-minded, with her tear-filled eyes, her insignificant, veiled face like a blind woman's, her gentle, soft hands and her belly tilting forward. Beyond her it was all emptiness; our garden, which was perched at the very summit of the rocks, tumbled down towards the azure sky, the waters of the Vézère and the village rooftops.

Our church shone in the sunshine. It was a former monastery chapel, with thick walls pierced by narrow windows like arrow-slits. But the thing which commanded my attention was the presbytery, which I had caught only a glimpse of the night before. It seemed very ancient, with its lintelled windows and its substantial stone roof. As I was alone, I decided to get to know it better.

On the ground floor was the kitchen, where we had drunk our coffee. The dominant feature was a vast fireplace, which filled the whole room with smoke. I pushed open a little door beside a cupboard, and was surprised to see that it led into a stable, occupied by a sparse flock of bleating sheep. I found log-piles and a kind of forge.

A flight of stone steps led up to the first floor. The previous evening, as I got ready for bed, I had noticed a large, beautiful seashell in my room, and some naval swords, bows and arrows piled up under a dressing table. Did my priest have a nostalgic longing for the sea? I opened the door to his bedroom; the thing which struck me particularly was that there was no bed, just a pile of blankets in one corner. Nearby, I found exactly what I might expect to see in the way of basic conveniences and piety, except for some more weapons, hanging from nails on a wall, and several collections of butterflies. I noted also that there was no clock, calendar or newspaper; in fact nothing at all to tell you the time of day or the date.

The other bedrooms, further down the corridor, were used for storage. They were unusable and dark because of the piles of assorted objects accumulated by generations of parish priests. It would have taken several days to get to the bottom of the various heaps.

I opened the shutters of the first room I entered, so that I could see more clearly. It turned out to be a chaos of *prie-dieux*, desks, benches, broken chairs bowed beneath the weight of gaping chests of drawers, and pea-sticks, heaped so high they touched the ceiling.

In the second room, which had whitewashed walls like all the other rooms in the presbytery, I bumped into another chaotic jumble of furniture, chests and baskets filled with long-forgotten clothes. There, I found clothing for housemaids and priests, cassocks and heavy cotton skirts, lavender sachets, linen, sun-hats, and white "Bâteau" knickers, slit up the sides, as worn by the Young Ladies you see on a Sunday morning, lifting their skirts behind country churches, while the bells are ringing for Mass. I counted more than fifty pairs in one trunk, all clean and new. Further on in a willow basket, I found faded skirts, soldiers' uniforms, theatrical costumes; enough clothes to dress myself a thousand times over. Near to a nice little cradle, a picture of the *Burial of Christ* was rotting away in a corner, and a swarm of maddened wasps was buzzing ceaselessly inside a wardrobe.

The third bedroom was used as a drying chamber for corn cobs, which had been laid out on the floor. I was going to close the door without going in, when I realised that these corn cobs had been arranged to form a number of perfectly geometrical shapes: circles, squares, suns, and more complicated figures, structured according to gradations of colour, which must have taken my priest several days' work and infinite patience.

The final room, at the far end of the corridor, was used purely as a drying-room for tobacco. Bunches of long tobacco leaves hung from the ceiling, and their sweet, pungent scent impregnated the whole house.

A ladder and trapdoor provided access to the attic,

which covered the whole of the first floor. The glimmers of sunshine which filtered between the stone roofing-slabs and the traceries of beams and laths cast an almost adequate light on a scattering of old books on the floor: the complete Virgil, *Lucretia*, Ovid's *Metamorphoses*, Cervantes, a copy of Plutarch's *Lives of Famous Men*, devotional texts. Rotting portraits of priests, stored away without their frames, looked at me with their large, wide eyes, like judges who were either benevolent or stern, meek or evil, watching me, following every move I made. That made me feel awkward for a while, I couldn't do a thing without them immediately swivelling their eyes towards me.

I was reading, sitting comfortably—or as comfortably as one could in a stuffy roof-space—when I heard someone climbing the ladder. My priest pushed open the trapdoor with his head. He did not see me, for it took several seconds to get used to the semi-darkness of the attic. I did not move. A delicious anxiety clutched at me. He climbed up the last few rungs:

"For God's sake, are you there?"

No reply. So as not to have climbed up for nothing, he set about removing the dust which covered the old books, striking the volumes with the flat of his hand, so frequently and so hard as he grumbled to himself that he stumbled and fell on top of me:

"Ah!" he exclaimed, "so that's where you were." Yes!

I told him, in the same tone of voice. But could he see my smile? Already he was pulling me towards him. As I was on my knees, he too knelt down to give me a good thrashing. After taking most of my clothes off, he struck me roughly, as he had struck the books. Did I weigh heavy in his arms? He made me get up and lie down across a low beam which ran across the attic; then, pushing my head down, he finished beating me in comfort. After that he went away, leaving me half-naked, panting, covered in sweat, my flesh burning against the rough beam. Once the trapdoor had closed, I regained my senses, telling myself that my fate was not really cruel, that the boys of Ancient Rome had undergone the same punishments and had not died; at last, rather cheerfully, I got down off my beam with my dust-blackened knees and my scarlet torso, put my clothes back on and went back to reading Plutarch.

By the time I too left the attic, I could tell from the silent house that I was alone again. I went into my room and washed myself in cool water, which took the entire contents of my little water-jug, as I was so dusty. Then I rested my elbows on the window ledge and gazed out at the trees and the sky. Birds were singing, hens were pecking around in the yard; a fine, strong smell of weasels drifted up from below. Worn-out from the beating I had endured, and feeling feverish, I was drawn by the calm of the garden.

At the far end of a pathway was a little murmuring spring, where I drank. In those early days of June, I found the power of the growing plants exhilarating; the scent of the carnations and roses troubled my young flesh. The warm air caressed my face. Evening fell. A sound of violently rattling saucepans told me that my priest had returned. A few logs tossed into the fireplace suddenly crackled and burned all at once. After he had called me two or three times, and since I was mischievously refusing to reply, he appeared in the kitchen doorway, which was all lit up by flames, his tall, thin silhouette stark against the firelight. Finally he came towards the clump of leafy vegetation where I had hidden myself. From my hiding place, among the leaves of a box tree, I saw his hand feel around for me, and finally encounter my face.

"Right", he shouted, "get into that house. I'll teach you to disobey me, you cheeky young..." How had I offended him? We left the moonlit garden and I followed him up to my room, where, after tying me across a chair, he thrashed me with a switch. Then he knelt down next to me and—as peculiar as ever—covered me with caresses, tenderly rocking me in my rush-covered clothes. He put out the light and remained there, beside my chair, in perfect darkness, saying nothing, kissing my face, for a whole quarter of an hour, before freeing me from my bonds.

It was at least nine o'clock in the evening when we decided to go back downstairs. We had a swift supper of coffee, lentils and biscuits, then I went up to bed.

My room had a narrow window which opened out onto the trees. My cool sheets smelt good. Unusually sweet bird-calls echoed in the branches. The birds' cries mingled with those of the tree-frogs in the garden pond, who were equally preoccupied with love and seduction. The green countryside sang beneath the starry sky. Other tree-frogs called back, from far away, their songs unspeakably loving and lingering. From time to time a whole section of the countryside would fall silent; in another, the songs would continue, then stop, then begin again, never tiring. Their calls kept me awake. Lying in my bed, I breathed in the perfume of the flowers which the night's spell had brought to life. The beautiful June sky shone, filled with stars; scents of pollen and roses floated up to me from the garden. I could not bear to stay in bed. Quite apart from the fact that my back was burning, I did not feel the slightest bit sleepy; on the contrary, I felt like plunging into the deepest depths of the cool greenery and shadows.

Barefoot, and as silently as I could, I tiptoed down the presbytery stairs. I opened a door. I felt as though I was walking out into a paradise of trees and flowers. Our dark stone roof stood out starkly against the sky. The calm surface of the pond gleamed in the shade of the pine trees. White flowers shone in the moonlight. I walked on slowly, following the light-coloured pebbles of a garden path, in the splendour and stillness of the night, until I reached a mass of thousands of green leaves and plunged in, cooling down the weals which burned my back and flanks, rubbing my flesh for a long time against this bed of greenery. From time to time the flutter of a bird's wing in the darkest depths of the foliage made my heart pound. The ewes in the stable jostled against the wooden walls; the occasional sounds they made, in the very special atmosphere of the night, were punctuated by matchlessly seductive silences. These made me want to pleasure myself, and I did so before collapsing into the low branches, which were kind enough to catch me.

After exciting myself in this way, and feeling a little weak, I returned to the presbytery, hoping that my parish priest was sleeping soundly.

My window was set deep into the wall and, in the morning, I settled myself down on the sill. From this calm, cool recess I could look down towards the north and see one side of the church. The previous evening's supper had not satisfied my appetite, and now a whole host of things served to sharpen it: the sun riding high above me, rays of light, the brisk air, a section of hillside which I could just make out, and all the fun I was promising myself while I was living with my priest.

There was nobody in the garden. I could clearly make out the rows of peas, and a stream with its network of irrigation channels. At that hour of day, my priest must be out doing his rounds. I went down and cut myself some bread, putting the chunks into my pockets. For the time being I could see nothing else to eat in this worse than poor house. I was beginning to suffer from hunger, and to realise to my astonishment that this deprivation gave me just as much pleasure as my priest's unjust punishments. In fact, if I wanted to be better fed all I had to do was attend to my own needs, since in that month of June the kitchen garden was positively bursting with peas which nobody ever picked, with cherries and with delicious, ripe strawberries which I could gather every day. I was considerably strengthened by this discovery, and by the pleasure I would undoubtedly derive from raiding the garden. In this happy state of mind, and in my imagination already full of cherries, I also convinced myself that several of the locked cuboards in the presbytery would contain excellent foodstuffs, hidden away inside.

It was not terribly difficult for me to find keys which opened almost all of them, hidden here and there. I found nothing to eat, but in one cubbyhole I did happen upon this strange object: a wooden stump about a metre tall, with four branches, inexpertly carved to resemble arms and legs. At the upper end of this log was a roughly-carved woman's head, topped by a straw wig. A few details had been added, in pencil. Was this my priest's woman? It wore a red rag instead of a skirt. Someone had burned incense before this horrendous idol, in a collection of sea-shells. Not quite sure what to make of this discovery, I locked the cupboard again, and put the key back into a little pot on the kitchen shelves. I was exhilarated by this unusual house, which drew me out of myself, troubled me and changed my character to the point where I felt I could do anything without blushing, and I would have stolen money if I had found any. I confined myself to raiding the tobacco drying-room for dried leaves, crushing them into powder in a handkerchief, ready for smoking, and hiding a kilo in a corner, for my own personal use.

My excellent parish priest arrived on the dot of noon,

as I was eating cherries. I saw him climb the steps; he was tall, broad-shouldered, narrow-hipped. With rapid movements he changed his shoes, pushing the bad-smelling ones under a kitchen dresser, and taking out a fresher pair. In tune with his usual habit of never staying in one place for long, he was already preparing to leave again; and on the principle that just the once would do no harm, he suggested that I should accompany him.

So we went round the farms together, on the pretext of collecting money for the poor. We were offered drinks everywhere, a polite excuse for not giving us anything else. Soon the farmyards were not vast enough for our uncertain steps. We visited seven or eight families, sitting down at the dark wood tables that smelt of cheap wine and bread, and having a drink. In the perfect mist of my drunkenness, I recall a girl of about twenty, who stayed crouched by the hearth all the time we were in her parents' house, and who told us flatly that she had nothing to give; she was beautiful, though her features were ravaged by the habit of sex-ual pleasure; I don't know whether she gave herself that pleasure, or had lovers, but everything in her expressed a profound knowledge of pleasure, violent, ferocious joy; in fact she looked just a little like me.

Apart from the keys to his church, my priest showed me keys to several presbyteries in parishes which he also served.

"My bachelor apartments," he told me, "come on, come on."

I remember an unknown village, our rapid, stiff steps, a blazing sun, our drunkenness which we tried to hide from a few old women who were knitting long socks on their doorsteps, a garden full of brambles and bees. He showed me into an old presbytery which he used as a house of pleasure. In the semi-darkness, with the shutters closed, he (. . .)* on the tattered couch of a priest's sitting room; as for me, I was drunk on cheap wine and coarse pleasure, and I let him have his way with me; it caused me less discomfort than the bad treatment I was accustomed to, and I fell asleep on the carpet, as soon as he had finished taking his pleasure.

When it was time to go back home, my priest said: "You haven't seen everything". Evening was drawing on and as there was not time to take me to his other bachelor apartments, he led me under a golden sky to ruined farm-buildings that stood at the foot of a little meadow, looking as if they ought to tumble into the stream. These were his too; he had inherited them. He grabbed my arm, picked a bunch of stinging nettles, opened a door, and closed it behind us. Here he is, whipping me with nettles, gathering his strength; here am I, crushed with tiredness and pain, leaning against a chest of drawers in a dead room, a bedroom with no

*There is a gap in the text here.

bed, strewn with the wreckage of the ceiling. I can make out nothing but a clock that has stopped, a ploughshare, a chair with the stuffing hanging out, a drawer jutting out of a chest, which I slide out a little more so as to get a better grip. And all the while I fear that my priest will move around too violently in this ramshackle house and bring down what remains of the ceiling on our heads, or that he will go through the worm-eaten floorboards and fall down into the cellar.

Afterwards we retraced our steps, brushing the patches of dust and plaster off our knees. My kingdom, he said to me, referring to the presbyteries and the ruined farms, whose keys he jangled in his deep pockets.

Back at his house, he gave me bread. Affectionately, almost fraternally, he pushed a goblet of wine towards me to restore my strength after the exhaustion of following him. It was a peaceful evening, and a deliciously cool breeze wafted in from the garden. I was so worn-out, so filled with delight that I lost consciousness the moment my head hit the pillow; plunging into a deep, admirable sleep, the best sleep of my life.

THE NEXT MORNING, I was alone as usual. Once again he had left me to my own devices. I wondered if he was at confession, and if he was, whether he would confess everything. I had a suspicion that he, and other young priests of his ilk, liked to share the revelation of their sins, only confessing them among themselves. As for my priest, if I was right about him, he simply wouldn't admit anything, not even to his colleagues. And so that morning of my life was entirely taken up with speculating about my priest. I saw nothing beyond the present moment, never imagined for a second that happiness was waiting just around the corner; or that it was already heading straight for me. Did I have any idea of what was about to happen? Didn't I have the faintest inkling?

The sun's glorious rays were burning off the dew in the garden; but the whitewashed walls of my bedroom remained in limpid shadow, as transparent and cool as an expanse of blue water, reflecting the sky. The shadow derived from the church, the house's north-facing aspect, and the dampness welling up from the spring, so liberally that it rotted the floorboards and turned the walls green much to the delight of the nettles which love old gardens and priests. The clear June sunlight had roused me from sleep, in that cold, silent house.

I went out. I saw the beautiful Sarladais. It was the start of haymaking. In faraway meadows reapers were hacking down the tall green grass; beside the trees, men were beating iron blades or sharpening their scythes, and the echo of hammer-blows made the rocky cliffs ring all along the Vézère.

I sat down on the church steps, laying my Latin books beside me. Our church stood among low walls of fallen stones, a favourite haunt of snakes. A maze of paths led down from it to the village, and it dominated the hillside, looming over it like a bird of prey. The people of the eleventh century were strange folk, and the carved stone pediment might well provide ideas for any boys who lacked them.

I read for a while. A boy aged around thirteen saw me, registered surprise and leant his bicycle against a wall. Was he going to give me the loaves he was carrying, or leave them in the doorway of the presbytery? He untied the strings which fastened the big, round loaves to the luggage rack.

"Give me the bread," I said.

I took in his manner, his grace, the smile on his lips. Spring had never created anything more delightful. He rummaged in the leather satchel at his hip, and took out a notebook and a pencil, licking the point delicately with the tip of his tongue.

"It's for my accounts."

He picked a few cherries:

"So. You'll be around then?"

"All summer," I replied, just as disconcerted as he was.

He left without further ado, and without paying much more attention to his accounts.

I made enquiries about the child, and learned from my priest that he delivered bread to us twice a week. A few days later, when ours was starting to go stale, I was sitting reading in front of the church while maddened bees buzzed about, frantically searching for pollen. That was when I got my chance to speak to him again. He lived in the village and delivered bread to the surrounding district. How I devoured him with my eyes, how passionately I hoped for a joyful outcome! Oh please, I begged silently, let him be bold, let him come quickly to me. I had no idea that my desire could be shared so instantly, or that love was already uniting us with that supreme facility it possesses whenever it wants to.

It was a fine, hot day. On the wooded horizon, ribbons of smoke curled up to meet the sky. Hayricks and men toiling in the fields heralded the full force of high summer. After the shortest possible hesitation, and without any acknowledgement passing between us, we set off together across the verdant countryside, in the direction of a little valley close beside the river. A vast cavern had been hollowed out by prehistoric floodwaters, and its coolness drew us inexorably, watched us walk together into a dark passageway, at the far end of which I could hear a little spring bubbling among the rocks. Stumbling in the gloom, we lit matches; but each went out more quickly than the last as we moved further and further away from fresh air. The last glimmer of daylight disappeared and we continued on together, across the faintly damp floor of the cavern. I took his hand. I love you, I said. I love you too, he replied. We fell into each other's arms. No embrace was ever sweeter or more passionate than ours. He tasted of love, given and received. I heard him stammer softly in the rock-hewn silence, and then his lips opened like a delicious flower, claiming my most enduring kisses. We went outside and saw that the spring we had heard, emerged in front of the entrance to the rocky hollow, where it became a stream. The boy did not utter a word. Happy to have found this pure water which had flowed so close by us, though it was so far from the cave, he drank long and deep.

Then he gave me an affectionate smile, squeezed my hand and went off to finish his deliveries. I lingered in the meadow where the stream flowed, feeling slightly drunk, breathing in the scents of hay and young grass. I did not move from that spot all day, as though I were in a state of grace. When night fell I returned home to my priest.

I now thought of nothing but the child. Early morning

was the moment that best matched the vigour of our burgeoning love. I was sitting reading in my priest's garden, a finger marking my place between the pages of Caesar's *Commentaries*, when I thought I caught a glimpse of him on one of the village paths. Unable to sit there and wait, I went after him. I thought I could recognise the scent of him, here and there as I went, as if the light breeze had not quite dispersed it. In the shadows cast by the rocks, the meadows mirrored the cool freshness of his lips. The mere thought that he had passed this way was enough to make my heart pound in my chest. An unerring instinct was guiding me towards him.

I found him asleep, lying beside the stream in that little valley we knew, the one people called the Devil's Valley. His bicycle was lying in a ditch, and two or three round loaves were still tied to the luggage rack. I walked towards him. Blackbirds were singing. All around us, thick brushwood alive with birds banked up towards grey rocks that stood out starkly against an intensely blue June sky. Buzzards circled lazily overhead. In the green grass, still soaked with dew, young snakes lay intertwined. He slept. There was scented pomade on his hair; and a trace of tiredness that tensed the muscles in his lovely face. He slept with one hand open, that little hand which I had already held in mine, which seemed to be waiting for me with all the power of love, and the simplicity of friendship.

I sat down beside him. There was something of myself in his mannerisms, his face; we shared the same sex, hence my happiness on that peaceful morning. I took his hand and slowly squeezed it.

"I was asleep," he said.

"Yes, you were asleep and I woke you."

I was perfectly aware of the power of my words. It seems to me that I seduced him by the sound of my voice alone. Even in completely innocent circumstances, I spoke a completely different language to the one he was used to hearing. My voice, which was a little hoarse, unsettled him and imposed my will upon him. The emotion I felt when I was with him helped me to change the tone, without even trying to. I spoke to him in an unfamiliar way which uprooted him from his own self and his way of life.

"I haven't finished my deliveries."

"I know."

He stood up. We walked into the darkened passageway where we had been before. In the silence and the darkness of the earth, I said: Where are you? My hand sought out his face, the sweet softness of his lips. We reached what must once have been a bend in the river: I love you, he whispered. And then he fell into my arms, overwhelmed, like our voices in that passageway. In the full light of day he was so in control of himself, a little sly even; but here he showed his true nature, and it was tender and passionate. He was exhausted after delivering the bread, and tiredness seemed to have made him a little drunk. I adored him all the more because, since I could not see him, he was the very image of my heart's most secret desires. I am your little girl, he said. Everything about him delighted me. He was more like a girl than a real girl; he acted out the role enchantingly against the mysterious backdrop of the cave. I seized him by the hair, and pushed him gently against the damp, cold rock; in the silent passageway, where I could hear the sound of waters bubbling under the earth, I truly believed that I was embracing love in its purest form, and I could have died of happiness.

Once we were out in the meadow again, all his boyish masculinity returned, and with it his courage and his nobility. I made no mention of the little girl he had claimed to be; he must come to appreciate that I could speak both to his soul, in the depths of the cavern, and at other times to the boy in him. He took a knife from his pocket, cut deeply into one of the loaves, and handed me a piece of bread.

"Eat this in remembrance of me."

Consecrated bread could not have moved me as much.

When I got back to my priest's house, I sat in the shade of a wall. Arrow-slits defended our church, which had no other opening save a narrow doorway. Two knights sitting astride a single horse, carved into the grey stone, offered ample proof that this was a Templar building. The nice, respectable parish priests would have shuddered with horror if they had raised their eyes a little higher to examine the strange sculptures just under the roof. Even without those abominations, everything about this place proclaimed a fierce determination to express the scandalous opinion that Man was made for Man, and not for Woman; that Woman is the Enemy. I was discovering the true mysteries, the true joy. The whole area was marked with the stamp of the Knights Templar. Crows soared over the rocky cliffs, full of secret lairs and tunnels; a potent magnetic force emanated from the immense hills, covered with undergrowth and chestnut saplings. The countryside was ablaze in the June sunshine; the hay was being brought in under rocks ploughed and shaped by the waters. The summer heat, the shrill cries of insects in a land swarming with snakes, all inflamed my love for this child who, like a freshwater spring, gave himself without a word.

A summer storm thundered down onto the forest out of a cloudless sky. We were intoxicated with summer. The child felt it, just as I did. A Europe of harvests, caves and boy sodomites filled my blood with abominable thoughts. The church's cool interior gave me respite from the violence of the day. When my eyes had grown accustomed to the darkness I sat down in a pew and opened a missal. I loved Latin; the virile strength of the language was in step with my passions, with my pounding heart. I was young; it pleased me not to be disturbed in this little church where nobody ever came, and to be able to dream of my love in peace. And yet I was afraid; the storm which was rumbling in the distance could not signify anything good.

FOR A FEW DAYS our life was wonderful. He belonged to no one but me; and no one suspected a thing. In the cave I worked him as one might work a piece of clay, a charmingly cool piece of clay. What a delicious task that was in the fierce summer heat! All the time the men were bringing in the hay, I was adoring a child in the depths of the earth. He was born in my arms to the accompaniment of my voice, almost singing with joy. At the end of the passageway I awakened him to full knowledge of himself; and his little mouth babbled tearful thanks in the darkness of the cave, where he freely expressed his need for loving caresses and embraces. One day, I struck a match so that I could see him; stripped of its outer covering, his whole body shone white. His clothes were round his ankles; it was the most radiant sight imaginable. The boy was standing at the well-spring of life, shuffling his feet on the cave floor, drunk, wordless, unhurried, very far from the light; and he was dancing. I struck a second match to see him again, but blew it out almost immediately, blessing the darkness which flung him into my arms.

We went outside, passing from delicious darkness to the hot air and blindness of the mid-afternoon. My greatest wish would have been never to return from that place, and to spend the rest of my life in the cave.

SOMETIME around the twentieth of June, I was eating with my priest:

"The police are in the village," he said.

My heart stopped in its tracks. "It's a terrible story," he went on. "Seems a twelve year-old boy has been offering his body to some local man. No one knows who. They're questioning the child at the moment, giving him a good thrashing, in the end they're bound to make him say what they want."

I felt as though someone had just struck me on the head with a stick, as though I were about to die. We were sitting at the table. There was bread in my mouth, but I couldn't swallow it. I saw myself in prison. At this very moment the one I loved must be suffering too, and suffering terrible violence! I imagined his panic, the terror of being interrogated. The first lightning-bolt had struck him, but the second would be directed at me. I left; I crossed the sun-burned fields of corn without even seeing them. The insects' cries pierced deep into my heart; the anguish which had taken hold of me at the table became a sharp pain which had entered my chest for ever and which fear kept reviving, like repeated stabs from a knife. That evening I would be arrested, I had no doubt of it. The storm was still thundering far away. All the brutality of the earth was revealed to me; those peasants, beating iron under the rocks, those ears of corn, those horrible insect cries. The thunder's rumblings echoed off the grey cliffs, riddled with holes where the crows nested. I walked along the river. Delinquent, I repeated to myself over and over again. My highest joy was reprehensible, against the law. At last I fell into a ditch, like a blind man, like a drunkard.

I had to go back. In my current state all I could do was go to the church. I opened the nail-studded door, its rough boards blackened by some unknown fire. I saw candles and a catafalque, made ready to receive a dead body; I climbed up to the altar, opened a prayer-book used by the choirboys, and read this sentence: *Sanctum et terribile nomen ejus, initium sapientiae timor Domini.* Murmuring the orison calmed my pain. Then I took great strides around the empty church. The coolness of the vaulted space where my footsteps rang on the paving stones reminded me of the cave. I washed my face in the coolness of a holy-water stoup. Had someone spied on us? Who had guessed the secret of our love? He too could count himself dead and buried. The child had felt the storm building up. The previous day, in the meadow, he had looked at me with a kind of wild passion, squeezed my hand with a tenderness that was almost painful, and taken his leave without showing his fear too clearly, sure of himself, still believing that he could lie to his family. At this moment he was having to answer for himself not to his family but to the *gendarmes*. Our village had had to call in reinforcements from the police station in a neighbouring small town; I imagined the terror this twelve-year-old child must be feeling, seeing the *gendarmes* who had come to the village because of him, making enquiries. Did they promise him forgiveness, if he accused me of shameful acts? Did they threaten him with the House of Correction if he deceived the *gendarmes*? What did he know of laws, and paternal Power?

The June solstice moon flamed over the hills.

I could be arrested. I decided to avoid prison through magic, to ally myself to my eternal soul; I scolded myself for letting time pass without taking steps in this regard. Swiftly, very swiftly, I ran down to the river. Thick clumps of mysterious, tall trees grew under the rocks where the shadows and the waters had slept together since the beginning of time; box trees which had rotted because of the floods, and because the sun's rays never reached them. I was young, which is pleasing to the spirits. After almost meeting my death in the clay, and just managing to extricate myself from a mixture of dead leaves and mud, I took a candle in my hand and approached a natural pool filled by a spring which entered it drop by drop. I saw my face in the water's mirror. A smile came to my lips, a smile in which cunning vied with the joy of seeing myself, knowing that I was eternal. I stirred the surface of the water with my hand; my face was wiped away, only to reform when the mirror settled down again. I blew on the water, I vanished but came back to life a few seconds later. I began again, blowing all the air out of my lungs, until I was almost dying, losing my breath. I drew my soul out of my body, and without opening my mouth again I walked swiftly away from the spring.

After doing as I have said, hiding my soul in the water's mirror where the Lawyers would not think to look for it, sheltering my true self from legal proceedings, I went back to my priest.

THE NEXT DAY I spent sitting by the hearth, poking the fire. The police inquiry had begun again, I knew that, but I also knew that the child had confessed nothing, and that I could stave off the danger which threatened me through magic. As evening approached, my priest took me with him to pull up some nets on an island upstream of the village, which lay across the river's course. We rowed across the turbulent waters of a sound and dragged our boat up onto the pebbly shore at the tip of the island which, I might add, seemed barely negotiable because of the thick undergrowth which covered it. When we had removed the fish from the nets, he took a whip out of his pocket and dragged me into the trees. I was aroused, all my senses heightened, noticing here a rotten tree-stump, there a smell of dead leaves, or a softness in the air. The river flowed past on either side of the island, swiftly, with little lapping waves. No place seemed to meet his requirements. After roaming about in the undergrowth he made me lie down, bare-chested, on a tree-trunk thrown there by the floods. I lay there with my hands over my eyes, determined to show how brave I was, yet trembling; but I heard nothing save the sound of fluttering wings, and then the unexpected crackle of little twigs snapping. I opened one eye; he was breaking off the branches around him, which would have got in his way as he beat me. Finally the first blow came, then others followed. He stopped at the fifteenth, not daring to go on. You're bleeding, he admitted, a little ashamed of having treated me so brutally. Proud that I had done no more than moan under the lash, I replied in a singsong voice that I deserved more than a hundred. We left the island.

He put the whip back into his deep pocket. Once we had crossed back over the river, we climbed back up to the presbytery by a roundabout route, so as to avoid going through the village.

That same evening, I ventured beyond our garden, right up to the very top of the rocks, and a little clearing amid the dry grass drew my gaze; you could not wish to see anything more charming, or more attractive. I thought I was dreaming: the child was following me up the paths and he was smiling at me in that triumphant way of his, showing me his gracefulness and his taste for doing exactly as he pleased. "I love you more than myself," he said, sitting down on a Fairy Chair hollowed out of the rock. He showed me two seats, hewn into the greyish stone. "See, this is your place and mine, since forever." I was charmed by his words. The air was soft and golden on the hills of the vast Sarladais.

He spoke again.

"Things are going badly."

"Did you talk?"

"I lied. If it goes wrong I'll save you."

"How?"

He smiled slyly. I knew he was very clever, and I was no less so myself. Supplications and responses for the use of the police were slipped into the coming night like the soft chirrup of a bird. When we had settled on our plan of action, he stood up and vanished into the bushes, amid the evening shadows.

I walked slowly back. I was about to pick up the keys, which were hidden under the brambles, when a blaze of light in our garden so astonished me that it stopped me in my tracks. Completely unaware that I was standing a few feet away from him, my priest lay prostrate in the grass, worshipping a standing stone, which was thrown into relief against the dark trees by the flickering flames of a little fire. His face wore an expression of extreme, inconsolable pain. Suddenly he threw himself backwards, with a loud shout which froze my blood. Then, with matchless tenderness and modesty, he pressed his lips to the stone which the dying embers summoned back into the darkened garden. Shoulders hunched, he went back into the house without noticing me. When I dared to show my face, he looked at me disapprovingly and prepared the supper in silence. What did he know of my love affairs? Did he suspect that I had witnessed his adoration of the stone? As we never talked about anything, I went up to bed.

Would I go to prison? After the cave, prison. Winter would come, the child would confess everything in spite of all our stratagems and I would be found guilty. I imagined life as one big game of Snakes and Ladders: cave, prison, river, church. Would I be in prison next winter, but only for a while, like in a board-game? I will save you: the child's strange words gave me hope without really reassuring me. Although fear still racked my heart, tormenting me as it had grown wont to do, I was now facing my situation with greater courage. Was I destined to escape prison, or on the contrary accept jail, that temporary death, like the earth which next winter would only pretend to die? I had loved spirits and springs, a cave had been my wedding chamber, could I really complain about my fate? Monks, sorcerers, barons of Périgord—they too had come into conflict with the law. I was sadly mulling this over when I was shocked by a frightful howling. What was my priest doing in the next room? I blew out my candle. Someone was knocking on my door.

"Come," he shouted, at the same time as I heard him running quickly down the stairs.

I got dressed. Shoving some bread into my pockets, I followed him into the woods. When we were a fair distance from the house, he discarded his priest's garb under the brambles and continued on his way dressed as a peasant. Reaching a lonely meadow, lit by the moon and stars, he cried out:

"Defend yourself."

Whatever did he mean? He picked up a stone, took a few steps back and threw it right at my face. Taking advantage of my confusion, my pain, and the blood which was gushing out of my mouth, he fell upon me. His fingers tightened around my throat and I lost consciousness. When I came to again, lying in the dew-soaked grass, he was holding my hand and sitting next to me.

"Come on, get up, I will save you," he said.

The same words the child had spoken: If things go badly, I will save you.

"I'm afraid for you," he went on. "Quickly, quickly, help me." His voice already sounded quite far away. Quickly, quickly, repeated the echoes, while I ran after him along the footpaths which criss-crossed the undergrowth.

We reached what had once been a garden. There, we lit a fire using planks and beams we found among the ruins. Soon a powerful blaze lit up the nettles and brambles, and the fallen stones. Kneeling, he stirred the embers with his bare hands. The fire's destruction of some beam or other liberated a red-hot iron ring; he retrieved it with the end of a stick, and hooked it onto a wall opposite us, where it continued to glow, slowly growing darker from contact with the cold stone, periodically pulsing fiery-red again, like a supplication.

I thought I would die of fear; a second ring lay shining on the burning coals, this one was toothed, for without realising it I had thrown the remains of a cart onto the fire, and this was the pawl.

"Go on, pick it up."

I hesitated, and he seized me by the hair.

"I said, take it."

Which I did, hanging it next to the first, on a nail where it gradually lost its fierce heat, progressing from transparent to vermilion red, blood red and finally reddish-black. With its pointed teeth it looked like a far-off sun, the most terrifying and the most radiant sight possible, shining over the whole of the Sarladais whose woods stood out darkly against the night sky.

"There, behind you, in the garden, look."

From the ruins where we were sitting, a few stone steps led to a very old orchard, lit up by the flames from our fire. An incredibly powerful, living presence was there, watching us in the darkness. I saw nothing.

"Look, under that apple tree." My gaze fell on a white flower in the wild garden, taller than the grasses and the brambles, young and beautiful, its petals opening wide to the night. The omen was good.

Aromatic smoke was billowing up from our dying

fire. Large clouds drifted over mankind as it slept. We were lying down beside the cinders, propped up on our elbows on the remains of a sort of paved yard. There was no urgency for us to return. He took off his jacket which he placed round my shoulders, and I pressed my body against his. The dying fire made it easier to see the ruins where we were lying; black stone roofs, green laurels, and the hills on the horizon, shining in the moonlight. He gently stroked my face, which lay against his chest, and that calmed me and made me feel better. This man, whom I thought of as common, was showing that he was noble and simple, full of friendship for me, that he would not reproach me for my conduct, or resort to useless violence. He gave me respite from myself and I was happy in his arms. Now, when my wild, affectionate nature was at its height, he soothed it, approved of its transgressions; I lay next to him and was plunged into a blessed state of unconsciousness and peace. There in that forest, this sense of primitive brotherhood overwhelmed me with happiness; it reunited me with the deepest, most ancient part of myself, the part which I loved the best. His broad, long hands caressed my lips; among the shadows and the trees, aromatic woods, almost consumed by the fire, intoxicated my senses. I was now no more than a spirit in the arms of my priest. My loneliness was banished. He placed my head on his knees, like the body of a newborn child who is being rocked to sleep. With my eyes closed, I heard nothing but his whispering voice, nourishing me with tenderness, curing me of my fears now that criminality separated me from other men. He spoke to me in words I could not understand, but which pleased my soul; then there was nothing but silence.

I opened my eyes. Intensely white, transparent clouds were passing across the dark blue night sky. There was a chill in the air. An owl hooted. We stayed there for a long time without moving, without saying a word. We were happy in the woods. He got to his feet: "Come on," he said. "Let's go home."

IN THE MORNING, still tired from my night's exertions, I took some firewood from the stable and threw it into a pile in front of the hearth. Rain had blotted out the countryside. The weak daylight which filtered in down the chimney lit up the firedogs and the cinders, so that they seemed immaculately white. And when I laid the flat of my hand lightly on them, I experienced the soft touch of those pale, pure cinders, which had the fragility and unspeakable gentleness of true love. I left the imprint of my fingers in that fine, hot, Paradise-white powder. I did not strike a match, or light the fire; I sat on a little bench and drank cold coffee, watching the rain fall like tears on my lost love.

Perhaps I could use magic not only to stave off all danger, but also to bring that beloved child back to me? We had a forge; I fashioned a kind of sword and beat it into shape with great hammer-blows. It was short, light, and twisted like a young snake, exactly as I had come to view the child. I threw it into the Vézère. I took my knife and plunged it into my arm, sawing through the flesh. At first it was just a deep gash which bled little; then my blood began to ooze out in large drops which fell into the river, whose grey, lively waters were carrying along a cargo of broken branches.

A few days later, by some miracle, I found my sword

further downstream, driven by the current towards the shingle banks. I covered it with kisses; I had found it again, after almost losing it in the tireless waters; I had rediscovered it steeped in the cool freshness of the river and my blood, as young and beautiful as the child who must now reappear and give himself to me as he had done before. I lived in a state of high expectation; I thought only of him, of his sweet madness in my arms, of his lips. Would he come? A different boy delivered the bread. I scarcely went out and dared not go down into the village. As it was no longer possible to go to the cave, I must search out an adequate hiding place for us here; I explored the presbytery, the sacristy, the church, and even a rather large wardrobe; the best place I could find was the staircase in the belltower, which boasted this advantage: no one could surprise us there because the stone steps echoed underfoot.

One morning, as rain was falling on the cinders, he entered the house without knocking:

"You're alone."

I smiled at him. He sat down next to me on my little bench, in front of the fireplace. He closed his eyes and took me in his arms. I kissed his sweet face, wet with rain, his tender, aroused lips. I made him some coffee, which he lapped out of a jam-jar which I used as a cup. He drank very little.

"You will come back again."

"Yes," he breathed, offering me his lips.

When he had gone I finished his coffee. And so he had come back. How good this cinder-coffee tasted. It tasted of love, it tasted of his lips, and it had the same sweet softness as the rain which fell on the big stone roofs and on the ricks of straw which stood rotting in the yards.

WE WERE NOT FAR from the village. One clear-skied evening, I recognised his bright, triumphant voice among the voices of the local children. It seemed he had deliberately steered their games on to the path which led to the church, so that he could proclaim his love to me. I hoped for more, that we could take up again where we had left off, this time on the staircase in the belltower.

Night was coming, and I dared not go back inside, for I was caught by the spell of that beloved voice. The moon rose above the green trees, still wet with rain; it shone among bright clouds. I was breathing in the scents of the garden, and dreaming of love, when my priest arrived home.

I prepared his supper, a task for which I had absolutely no aptitude. Although Nature had generously endowed me in other ways, in this respect she had left me poverty-stricken. I lit all the fires of Hell, put our best foodstuffs into saucepans, threw in some salt and pepper, and gave the whole thing a stir; I wasn't at all sure what the result would be. The thought of a delicious meal obsessed me every evening and, as we were poor, I was particularly taken with the idea of a meal made out of practically nothing which would, by some miracle, turn out to be the most exquisite thing in the world, and the very one capable of truly satisfying the hunger which tormented me. However I fared no better than on previous evenings.

We went up to his room and he closed the door behind us. There, in the darkness, he tied me across a chair in his usual way, holding me firmly in place and ensuring that I was his and his alone. For this purpose he kept a whole drawerful of ropes.

Whip in hand, he sat down next to me on another chair. With my trousers round my ankles, he began to beat me; I felt as though I was being well and truly devoured, that my flesh was coming away in shreds, that I was being roasted, that since I had not cooked anything good for supper, he was devouring me instead. He laid the whip across his knees; in the darkness I felt his hands on my naked flesh. He touched me as one might caress a woman, stroking me all over, his hands lingering between my thighs. For a while now I had been his maidservant, doing the things which I thought maidservants do, and which perhaps they do not; things which gave my priest far more satisfaction than any real maidservant could have done. Apart from having to prepare our spartan meals, I had to tidy the house and, some evenings, not only receive the whip, but also act the loving wife. This change in status pleased me, not because of any perverse streak in my nature, nor from any sexual weakness, for I was extremely masculine and proud to be so, but because I believed that this would allow me to acquire certain powers. Before beating me he slipped his arm about my waist, he whispered in my ear, and I felt the feminine part of me come to life. When alone, of course, I was from time to time my own wife, but without much belief in the role; whereas in the arms of my priest I was very pleased to find someone more or less crudely convinced by my dreams, thanks to the darkness, and who, in return, convinced me. On this occasion I had the feeling not so much that I was giving myself to him than that his caresses were enabling me to discover the other half of my being, myself as my own wife. My reasoning was more or less like this, namely that having my whole life ahead of me to act like a man, at sixteen I ought to see what a charming, sturdy, priest's maidservant I would have made. No other could match this one, intelligent in sexual pleasure, gentle and strong; I pitied her as she was beaten, and loved her all the more for it; when she was at the height of pleasure, I was astonished by it and admired her for the resilience it took her to bear so much joy; this dialogue with myself led to perfect happiness.

The darkness and the fear of the next blow made me alert to the slightest sound; I noticed a mouse scratching near the door. Through the closed shutters we could hear leaves whispering in the garden, shaken by the wind. Was it raining, as it did every night? He was gripping the whip firmly now, very close to my legs, so he could thrash them without pity; several of the thongs, weighted with little knots, dropped to the floor, and the sound they made as they fell was like the patter of a few little cherry-stones. He shook the whip to untangle it, so that he could use it more effectively; and so that I was in no doubt of the fact, he made all the leather thongs slap against the edge of the table; I was terrified by this, although less so than the books and pens which were laid out on the table-top. He lifted the scourge; then, as I have said, I had the feeling that I was being cooked, burned, that he was eating me for his supper, that I had been set on fire. I heard the whip-lashes whistle and slap against my skin; in the darkness the strokes sometimes fell on my shoes, and that gave me respite; others, better aimed, threw me back into the fire.

He had stopped beating me. The floor felt cold beneath me. Hindered by my bonds and burned by the scourging I had received, I recovered my breath as I leaned against the chair-back. We stayed like that for a long time. He was still sitting next to me, not speaking to me, not touching me, not seeing me. One side of my waist continued to throb with heat; a blow from the leather thongs had severely grazed my skin, and in the darkness I was suffering acute discomfort which slowly lessened. He released me from my bonds and, still without putting the light on, he lay down on the blankets in one corner of the room, which served him as a bed. Straightening my clothes, I went and lay down next to him. That corner of the room formed a sort of encampment; my hands encountered rumpled blankets, clothes, a hunting knife and some shotgun cartridges in a jacket pocket. What was he thinking about as he held me in his arms? As for me, a delicious exhaustion plunged me into a doze. I was happy in that little presbytery bedroom, my happiness derived from perfect complicity with my priest, who I guessed was equally busy with his dreams. Did he love me because of that fellowship which united us without us ever having to explain ourselves? The wind was blowing through the woods; I guessed it was raining a little; the mice were running along the passageway. In the darkness he pushed me gently away and crawled across the floor to one of the corners of the room; I heard him pick up a few objects and come back, bumping against the chair. He struck a match and I saw that he had brought a bottle of rum, a little metal teapot, and a spirit lamp, which he lit. He poured some rum into the teapot, added some sugar which he took out of his pocket, then returned to me on the pile of blankets where we had lain down: the lamp's little flame gleamed faintly; in the blackness we could not take our eyes off it. When the rum began to boil and sizzle, he leant over and threw in a lit match which went out instantly. He struck another, and a blue flame covered the surface of the rum. He pressed himself against me again and we waited. What time of night was it? I had no idea. An unquenchable tenderness for him made me squeeze his hand very tightly; he held mine hard enough to break it. I kissed his hand. The rain was taking over the garden. Swiftly pushing down the lid of the teapot he extinguished the rum, found some little glasses under the blankets, blew out the spirit lamp, and in the complete darkness held a boiling hot, sugary brew to my lips. Immediately I entered into a state of absolute wellbeing and became the loving, charming wife. That encampment of rumpled blankets took me back to the earth's first nights, to a state of nature, to all the chaos of primordial life. With my face nestling against my priest's fur-collared jacket, like the pelt of some beast, I felt drunk with pleasure, I felt hot. I liked this lair.

He caressed me with an exact knowledge of my flesh, with the skill of a bone-setter, not saying a word to me, for fear of drawing me out of my trance. His long hands seemed to know me perfectly; from head to toe, there was not a bone, not a muscle he did not mould with a subtlety which delighted me. He cured me of my loneliness as one cures a sprain. What gave me the most satisfaction was his knowledge of me, deep enough to give the impression that he wished to raise me to infinite, divine levels of pleasure, to hear me singing on my knees in his arms; deep enough to make it seem he had known me for all eternity.

I needed to sleep. I awoke around three in the morning, not wishing to stay with him any more, eager to go back to my own room. In the corridor, heartburn caused by the rum prompted me to go down to the kitchen and get some water. I was hungry; a curious need to loot everything in the house drove me to open the cupboards, I would have liked to steal, take, seize anything and everything. Sated with nothing but water, and with the idea that I had formed of my multiple existence, I went back to my room and fell asleep again, properly this time.

I LAY on the sea-bed and opened my eyes, delighted to see the light again. The pearly-white walls of my cold, damp, sunless little bedroom were rippled by movements of air like the shadows of waves; and this effect, together with the beautiful sea-shell on my bedside table, created an impression of deep, clear water. It was good to feel the sheets sliding coolly over my thighs. From the depths of this Ocean I saw the wild greenery of our bird-filled garden. Although I was no early riser, I left my bed without further ado.

If the absence of any clock or calendar had astonished me, by now I knew the house well enough to have established that there were no mirrors or looking-glasses either. Ecclesiastical modesty may banish modern comforts, but that doesn't prevent presbyteries containing at least one looking-glass, so that you can give your hair a decent combing; here, there was nothing of the sort, nothing which would allow you to see yourself; without a calendar I lived according to the seasons, without a clock, I used the colour of the air to tell the time; and without a looking-glass I did not wash myself, simply gave my face a quick rinse, nothing more.

In the kitchen I made myself some coffee. I was alone, as usual. My priest had left at daybreak. He only said Mass here once a year, or when somebody died. He merely lived here, having chosen this residence so as to be left in peace. Nobody came up to see us and I did not complain about that. Better to feel sorry for Monseigneur, the Bishop of Périgueux and Sarlat, whose only choice for running the parishes is between old priests, holy but impotent men, and young priests who are always gadding about the countryside and making tongues wag. As for mine, I would have preferred him to feed me better; he dined in his other parishes; from time to time he did not eat for three days, apparently without ill-effects, but my sixteen-year-old stomach could not get used to the regime. All he left me was enough to make a light snack: some coffee and sugar, in iron caddies above the fireplace, some bread, some biscuits; the sort of groceries an old woman might have. I didn't complain about this poverty, because the kitchen garden saved me. In June, sweet garden peas taste exquisite with bread.

Little stone walls enclosed our large kitchen garden. This had formerly been the cemetery belonging to a little community of monks, and all you had to do was disturb the soil to unearth bones. Our vegetable garden had been invaded by a jungle of green brambles, and here and there had been haphazardly dug over by my priest; but it flourished in the sunshine. What astonished me was the strength of the plants; do the memories of holy souls please growing things; do the dead exercise some kind of spell over them? For whatever reason, everything grew better here than elsewhere, and I have never eaten better strawberries than ours, grown on skulls.

Brandishing a baguette, I walked on through the buzzing of bees. The snakes terrified me. A grass snake slid over my bare feet and disappeared among the tall grasses. The surroundings of this former religious house now belonged only to the snakes. They twined round each other and slept in the sun. The snakes killed the birds. The snakes killed the frogs and toads in the pond. The snakes writhed about and shed their skin. They proliferated in the crumbling walls, they devoured each other; they became big snakes; they were cold. Cruel eyes followed my every step. That kitchen garden both attracted and frightened me.

I felt more at ease in the church, whose key I kept in my pocket. I opened the little narrow door. The dampness of the old walls, blotched with mildew, the darkness, and the stoup filled with cool holy water always made me feel as if I was entering a cave. A golden lamp with a red flame burned before the altar. I closed the door behind me. I loved the silent interior, with its vaulted roof and its paved floor, which made my footsteps ring out sharply. Narrow loopholes allowed light to pass through. The cavern-like stillness was no different to that of the rocky passageways

where I so often ventured; here was the same profound, shadowy darkness, the same smell of ancient
stone. It gave me pleasure to linger in the church. The
silence of the cool aisles, a lingering smell of incense,
that lamp burning before the altar lured me there every
day. In the sacristy we had a wardrobe full of albs, chas-
ubles of several different colours, like the seasons,
embroidered in gold and silver. Old dragons rubbed
shoulders with eternal vices, carved into the stone. I
loved the holy darkness where all I had to do was close
my eyes to see the child again. Summer carried me
towards him; the blue morning air, the river waters, the
shadowy caves, the weight of the rocks all filled me with
the desire to make love to him. I thought of nothing but
his lips, his arms tenderly framing my face.

Seven or eight centuries were represented in the
church, although the only remaining Norman parts
were the walls, the floor-tiles and the crypt. The carved
altarpiece dated from the eighteenth century; the elegant pulpit, in pale blue and gold with wooden panels
and prettily painted angels, from the seventeenth; the
roofing and the nave, from the fourteenth. It was on
this cross-section of time that my love depended. Indeed,
I was convinced that I had lived in this land before;
that in each century I saw my priest and the child
again, and myself with them. My probable brushes
with the Law, this bad business, happened to me in

every life. I was certain I had known the child before, in the time of the kings. It was our custom to meet up again every century. This impression of something which had lasted beyond a single life, this vast sense of time, flattered my love.

I climbed up the staircase inside the belltower, a winding spiral set into the very heart of the walls. Softly I pressed my lips to the stone where the seasons' dampness lingered, along with something at once icy-cold and burning-hot, the heat of summer, the winter freeze, the weight of the earth and the sky. I had told him of my plan to meet him here; what wouldn't I have given to hear his light footsteps on the flagstones? But I heard nothing beyond the very particular silence of the church, which no woman parishioner ever entered.

He had his own unique way of appearing: often, indeed, he allowed me simply to guess at his presence. Soundlessly he was there, a few steps away from me; turning round, I saw him smiling at me. He enjoyed surprising me like this. It was his way of telling me: See how cunning I am; and also a way of reassuring me about the consequences of this affair by reminding me, each time we met, that he was still very clever.

I climbed a little higher, and, through an opening in the wall, I glimpsed the beautiful Sarladais in the blue of summer. By pressing my face hard against the stonework I could make out one side of the village, fifty metres below me, the houses roofed with *lauzes*, flat stones laid one on top of the other; and I could see a loop of the Vézère. From the staircase in the belltower I commanded only a small section of the countryside, but it was beautiful and vast enough to hold my gaze indefinitely. I could see for a long way and the hills went on and on until they reached the woods, on which the summer heat weighed heavy.

At the edge of the river, so deep and green under the rocky cliffs, a fisherman was holding his line; another and his boat and their shadow were drifting slowly downstream. I had an almost vertical view of the Sarladais, which gave me a feeling of vertigo; almost on the vertical too were the village and the river, and a few cultivated fields. The only thing I saw normally was the horizon, the vast, seemingly empty horizon.

The Sarladais, also called Black Périgord because of its thick growth of small, dark oak and walnut trees, is a partially deserted land, planted here and there with fields of maize and wheat, and narrow tobacco plantations. It is a wild land and, for he who knows how to see, a land of spirits. A land of sorcerers. Templars, barons, priests, peasants, all practised the art to a greater or lesser degree, and the green and black Sarladais countryside, still echoing to primeval cries, retains a little of the souls of all those who were once magicians.

I loved this land where I had lived for four or five

hundred years, this land of ghosts, of cool caves and woods. I loved the summer which made me giddy with delight, I loved the sound the insects made, the way the crows wheeled in the skies overhead. I closed my eyes, then opened them again; once again I saw the beautiful Sarladais with its haystacks, its carts and its islands; the Vézère was still flowing along under rocky cliffs; the birds were gliding, the fisherman was casting his line, another man or the same.

I left the loophole, returned to the nave and sat down in one of the choir stalls.

Around the middle of the day, what better thing can you do than mull over your own passions? The innocence of the morning is no more than a memory, the heat stirs the blood. If I cross-examined myself, the strongest passion which burned in me seemed to be the attraction I felt for the power of growing things. Now, in early July, the plants' exuberance and insane proliferation appealed to me. Seeing the grass and the trees pleased and delighted me. Even in the stillness of the church the memory of them disturbed me. The more I lived at one remove from my own century, the more I found that I was unusually sensitive to the summer, which made me drunk with happiness and which found powerful resonances in my flesh. The thickness of the foliage, the inextricable tangling of grasses and brambles frightened me, so much so that I experienced a kind of delicious terror. Like the snakes, the trees and leaves fascinated me; I lived in a state of magic, and the beauty of the growing plants captivated me.

As for the child, I loved him with all the strength of summer. My whole being reached out to him. Like the light of noon which makes you close your eyes, the love which I felt for him blinded me and concealed the dangers I was running in wanting to see him again. A magical spell united us; it separated us from other men and it protected us from the distressing consequences of that love. The child sensed it; was it me he loved, or did he love that immunity, that spell, more than me? Whichever was the case, he had confessed nothing, we could see each other again here. Less good fortune would have seemed to me to indicate less love, and I would have withdrawn from the liaison, not through cowardice, but because I would have believed that a power had been broken.

Facially, I looked a little like him. This resemblance inclined me to see him as an immediately desirable being. We shared the same body heat, and that made me feel love for him. This facial and bodily resemblance intensified my feelings for him, my desire to make him mine, or at least to be loved by him. The way I handled him was calculated to give him pleasure exactly as he wanted it, so that through my actions he would instantly recognise me as an exact mirror of himself, only more skilful. I loved him because I did not know exactly who I was, and consequently nearness and resemblance immediately made me seek out myself. I had reached the point of believing that there is no love except in so far as one's unconscious strives to find itself in others, believing that there is no love except in delicious error.

Each day I passed the time as I wished. They say that idleness is the mother of all vices. Anyhow, I went back to the presbytery, around noon to judge from the height of the sun. I was thirsty so I drank some cold coffee diluted with water. I opened a drawer, took out a blue booklet of Job brand, non-adhesive cigarette papers, and went up to the tobacco drying room. Sitting on the bare floor, with my back up against a white wall, I reached into my pocket and took out my little store of tobacco, tightly twisted into a handkerchief. I rolled myself cigarettes which I smoked in that storeroom, which was so steeped in the scent of dried plants that it gave me a headache.

A heavy silence followed the sounds of morning. This was the sad stillness characteristic of the middle of the day, when the snakes and the shadows have disappeared. No more bird calls, just an impression of blinding light and immobility. The summer heat in that bedroom, the small amount of hard light which filtered in through the drawn shutters, and the violent smell of rotting tobacco made me want to stretch out

on the floor and sleep until evening. But I managed to
stay awake, for the ceiling beams, the wooden laths,
and the flaking plaster which revealed the layer of clay
and straw beneath, formed a curious abstract picture
which I could not take my eyes off; I found beauty in
those layers of dried earth, plaster and wood, which
smelt good impregnated with the scent of tobacco; I
found sweetness too, and a kind of tenderness in that
work of oblivion, degradation, chance, the changing
seasons, several centuries of abandonment, an expanse
of time as vast as my own.

I went into the next bedroom where, as you know,
my priest had created several patterns representing
suns, circles and eyes, through a skilful arrangement of
corn cobs. I would have asked him the reason for this
fine, patient work, if we hadn't agreed not to talk about
anything serious. That man dared not confess anything, or admit anything serious; he left the moment I
ventured to speak frankly. He kept silent about the
bizarre tastes I knew he had, tastes which were incom-
patible with the dignity of his office, though he showed
no desire to change either his office or his errant ways.
If I had dared to kick over the beautiful arrangement
of corn-cobs, he would not have reprimanded me, he
would not have explained anything, but I would have
found the door to the drying room closed and firmly
locked. The good side of this decision to keep silent

was that we could abandon ourselves entirely to our passions, without feeling constrained to consider them honestly, or debate them between ourselves. Similarly, I had difficulty in carrying on any kind of lengthy conversation with the child, because of the difference in our ages, which led effectively to profound silence; this difficulty disturbed me to the point of extreme pleasure and made me more attached to him with each day that passed. The distance which we had agreed to maintain between us was something which my priest desired because of a remnant of decency, a taste for secret things to which I was less attached than he, for I considered it perfectly possible to put everything down in writing. He showed that he was still a peasant through his determination to shy away from too much responsibility, and his opinion that silence covers everything, that it absolves everything, that the only irremediable thing is something that is written down; like the child who believed that impunity absolves everything, whereas on the contrary I would have liked to put everything down on paper, with the ulterior motive that writing justifies everything. So, for some time now, my priest had given up reading books; he regarded them with horror as though he could detect in my calm gaze an aptitude for the remembrance which he feared, too much joy to forget anything, and a taste for writing about it. He now read only works on sailing, whose straightforwardness he found reassuring; he never opened anything serious; he hid the penholders, he put water in the ink, through tight-fistedness, and through a desire for illegibility and transparency; he claimed that his only interests were vast sea-voyages, and the islands.

The early afternoon heat, a crushing, heavy heat which exhausted me, combined with the smell of tobacco and made me feel sad. I hated the middle of the day, the motionlessness of the afternoon, and that grey light filtering in from the garden.

I climbed up to the attic. I loved it with its arrangement of eighteenth century beams laid on top of each other in such a way that you would have thought they formed the ribs of an upturned ship. The flat, unevenly-laid stones of the roof-covering allowed rays of sunlight to pass through and, as always in attics, a delicious anxiety took hold of me. So as to read in comfort, I sat down on the floor. I showed a strong propensity to sit or even lie down on floors; even a relatively uninformed observer would have deduced the vice in my character from my refusal to use chairs, and would not have been far wrong, for I did indeed feel all-powerful impulses not to act like other people; the social graces and manners I habitually demonstrated did not hold out for long, as soon as I was on my own for a while I slipped back into my wild state.

In the old books which littered the floor, several of

which I had stacked up to rest my elbows on, I found cruelty mixed with clumsiness, skill, and flashes of honesty. Those books were well printed, bound with that same red leather which is used to make school whips, and radiated the good smell of old ink. Treatises on Greek versification, books of religious instruction burning with love, Latin tomes as strong as athletes' muscles, *galant* little books, I took pleasure in reading them all in that priest's attic.

I came upon Goya's *Caprices*, and I spent the heavy, painful afternoon looking again and again at the engravings which touched me to the quick. This European madness, that was my madness; the demons and the priests did not astonish me, nor did the anguish of prison, which I knew well. As I opened those books, the memory of several of my youthful lives came back to my mind; memories of provincial schools, priests' gardens, sunny springtimes beside calm rivers. Fragments of the Past which belonged to me enchanted me, and it pleased me to know that I had lived longer ago in that part of France than I would ever have believed.

I practised a curious method to give myself extreme pleasure, for I had noticed that a very large number of strokes of the whip plunged me into a powerful state of delirium, at the height of which I lost consciousness. I knew from experience that it is enough for the punishment to be given gently at first, so that the pain remains easily bearable; after which, beyond a hundred strokes, you no longer feel anything and can continue indefinitely. As long as you have a little courage and perseverance, you can exceed five hundred strokes, even vicious ones, with no other ill-effects beyond swollen, blackened flanks, and a little blood on your clothes; one side will be more affected than the other if you whip yourself, for the lashes twist and only strike one side. Then you become delirious, cast out of your own body.

At the far end of a room in the house I found a locked cupboard. On the back of the door, suspended from nails, hung whips, the kind you buy at fairs, some with red handles, others with yellow; old school whips, with handles of turned wood, like chair feet; and several whips which my priest had made himself, their long thongs tipped with knots. I knelt down on a *prie-dieu*. The habit of confession combined well with my peculiarities, with just one difference: contrary to the spirit of contrition I was not feeling remorse about anything, nor guilt for anything, only a violent and savage desire to suffer and to live. With the shutters and windows closed, I did as I have said. I whipped myself, half-naked, in that darkened room, on my knees on the prayer-stool, in a shadowy gloom which was the accomplice of my eagerness to mortify my own flesh. At the hundredth stroke I allowed myself a rest,

I was so exhausted I could do no more; I laid my face gently against the wall. The sounds of the countryside reached me distantly; peasants were travelling past in a cart; people were talking in the yard. I picked up the whip again; I was good to myself; I held back after the hardest strokes; I stopped beating myself when the bite of the leather gave me too much pain, for my courage did not exceed a little compassion for myself. And who could have guessed when it was necessary to spare me, who could have sensed when I needed pity, who better than myself, bleeding from my own blows? I beat myself hard, for a long time, so that each time I could give myself the joy of whipping gently when I had gone too far. I put all the heart into it that my semi-solitude allowed. Then I gave myself proofs of love and kindness, both of which were rather lacking in my life, until at last I fell to the floor, drunk with pity and tender self-love, after more than a thousand strokes.

I was jerked out of this solitary pleasure when a violent thunderclap shook the presbytery. There was a long silence and then I heard the rain coming, a powerful summer rain which drummed on the leaves and on the stone roof. So as to avoid the draughts which, people say, attract the thunder, I closed doors and pulled a few little windows shut around me. In the flare from a bolt of lightning, a second thunderclap sounded above the pine trees; a slow, stormy roll echoed all around before vanishing into the depths of the thick foliage. Our trees were shaking their branches; torrents of water were falling from our roof and making hollows in the earth at the foot of the walls, so deeply that the rain uncovered the stones in the garden. A curiously green light had replaced the brightness of day. A lightning bolt sheared the top clean off a cedar. The entire countryside growled ominously. The storm thundered with terrible detonations, and from time to time with slow tearing noises which originated high up in the sky, hesitated, then came swooping down towards our trees; more often the storm thundered heavily onto the village with a sound of logs being thrown violently to the ground. It went away, came back, frightened me. The river too received its fill of the storm; then it became noticeably weaker. There was no longer so much noise, and everything began to calm down. Silence came, broken by the fall of the last drops of water sliding down off the roof.

I ate some bread. That silence, that bread, the coolness of that part of the evening, mingled with the scents floating up from the rain-swept garden, all seemed delicious to me. I had to attend to my priest's ewes. We kept them in a stable which was entered by a door at the far end of our kitchen, and consequently we could hear them knocking their heads against that door, whimpering close by us like gently captive souls, their feeble squabbles, their murmurs often interrupting what little conversation we had. Behind that door they were born and died in darkness, on their thick bedding, dreaming of green grass. Their smell exuded the all-conquering sweetness of Limbo. Another stable door led out into the garden; I opened it each evening, and they showed pleasure as they walked out into lush meadows.

I followed them and sat down at the edge of a little wood. The storm forgotten, the moon's perfect disc rose into a translucent azure sky, setting it all aglow; beside it shone the night's other child, a single star twinkling over the Sarladais hills. The tangled tree-trunks were becoming difficult to make out. The air, now as cold as springwater, showered me with joy, touching my lips and my eyes. A bird sang among the black branches. I saw the bird clearly. Large, blue, crested, it emerged from the greenery with a sound of crumpled wings, and passed above my head with an insistent cry, heavy in its flight.

Our sheep went back when they chose to. They lingered late in the meadows, grazing under the low branches of the trees, and it was almost midnight when I heard them sneaking back along our garden paths. They ventured right up to windows of the house, knocking over the watering cans and chairs, before deciding to go back into their stable. So, paying them no further heed, I set off up the path which led back to the presbytery.

I needed nettles. We had some along our north-facing walls, in damp corners. Tall nettles lived there, along with the rushes which have a fondness for fresh flesh and the blood of young children. I mixed powdered, dried nettles with tobacco, and I found this blend suited me well, not for reasons of economy, for I was not short of tobacco, but because the smoke of powdered grey nettles had particular properties. Protecting my fingers with a handkerchief, I picked fistfuls, which I crammed into my pockets.

My priest had still not arrived home. Not particularly expecting him, or even wanting to see him for that matter, since I was greatly enjoying being alone, I went up to my room. I had no desire to put on the light. Sliding between the sheets, I laid my nettles under the pillow to dry, and peacefully smoked a mixture I'd prepared a few days earlier. Nettles have a scent redolent of plants, death, dreams, love and calm water under the moon; and they produce a rapid high. In my white sheets, with my eyelids closed, I smoked. I fell asleep; I forgot to smoke; nettles go out more quickly than tobacco; you have to draw in the smoke regularly to keep them alight; I lost consciousness with an acid taste of burnt sap on my lips; I felt that my soul was detaching itself from my body; I was becoming separated from myself, I no longer inhabited my own face, nor my eyes nor my arms, and I was standing some distance away from my physical self.

In this altered state I could detect in minute detail the secret movements of life, the growth of plants, the fermentation of stagnant waters, here an imperceptible movement of the air, there the crack of a branch. After our ewes had finished roaming up and down the garden paths, and silence was re-established, flowers opened and plums fell. A spell was at work. Like some magical being who left the sheltering greenery each evening to come up to our trees, that spell was making the night grass grow, the leaves open out and pods appear all the way up our pea-sticks. In the distance, beyond the little walls of our kitchen garden, the whole of the Sarladais was singing in the voices of the tree frogs, under the starry sky.

I wanted to see the plants growing and walk among the branches, to join with this garden spell which was calling to me. The darkness of the countryside terrified me. Indeed, I would have stayed in my bed, but the summons was becoming too urgent. I got up and dressed. However, because part of me was afraid, I took a long bayonet from the room next to mine. Among my priest's possessions were bows and poisoned arrows from Africa and Oceania, naval swords, Indo-Chinese daggers, Malayan knives. An indisputably

French bayonet from the 1914 war, which was not too rusty and slid quite easily out of its metal scabbard, seemed to suit my purposes. I stuck it through my belt and went outside, walking into the moonlight.

I saw a sky covered with stars. My steel blade gleamed; the sound of the Vézère reached my ears. Other low stone walls enclosed other gardens. Mankind's dwellings lay sleeping, their shutters closed. I distrusted and feared humans. Given a choice between the splendour of the night and the heavy sleep of men slumbering in the arms of their wives, deep in those big, soft country beds where people give birth or die in sweat and blood, I had chosen the night. Dogs caught wind of my scent and growled in their chains. The slow sound of the Vézère drew me on; to get to it, I decided to go through the woods rather than skirting the village.

I set off at a rapid, silent trot, diving in among the tall, cold grasses. My legs became soaked with night-dew, and my long bayonet left a furrow of crushed stems behind me, but I felt no tiredness and made rapid progress. The moon lit up little valleys; I walked through transparent shadows, banks of light, and I did not stop until I reached a meadow.

The second crop was growing in abundance between cliffs full of sheltered hollows overgrown with thick vegetation. The World was there before my eyes, the world of stars and leaves in the Great Time of the Night. The earth was turning slowly in a clear sky striped with pink clouds, pointed like the prows of boats. The rocks and the woods lived their real lives in the moonlight, far from men. And I lived my real life with them; I nourished my soul, I drenched myself with happiness, I drank in the strength of the World; this was reality, lasting and unforgettable. The fathomless, living presence of magical space imbued every leaf. Eyes wide open, I had only one desire: never to return to live among humans. Indeed, I was quickly forgetting them; there was not one fragment of my true being, of my real personality, which did not participate unreservedly in the eternal celebration of sovereign night.

A bird sang. Birds sing at night more often than people think. I loved that soul, whose language of love and joy I now understood. In the middle of the meadow stood a few trees, four, very close together, so that their crowns formed a single round, shining ball of leaves. The bird was singing there. I rid myself of my sword, laying it down in the grass. My mouth voiced tender calls, exactly like the bird's, and he answered me as if I was a bird. Then I prowled like an animal, here and there, among the grass, around the tree.

I wanted to go further. The waters of the Vézère flowed twenty metres or so below me. I would have entered the woods without further delay, to go down to the river, if a feeling of weakness had not held me back. I retraced my steps, picked up the bayonet, and instantly regained complete happiness; the steel and copper blade in my hands attracted forces which guided me in the semi-darkness, which protected me from the cold of the night, and which reassured me. Because of its weight, this blade also acted like a light pendulum, helping me to run. I left the light-filled meadows to plunge deep into dark undergrowth. I used my sword to break through the brambles, which snatched at my clothes, to forge a way through the densely tangled vegetation, to uncover faint paths leading to the river, whose mirror-gleam captivated me. It served me less to open up a path through the shadows and the sweet-chestnut shoots than to give me a better understanding of my most secret instincts; for I was choosing my path according to magic spells and fears. Here, beneath the branches, the gleam of light on water delighted me; there, some damp cave filled me with fear, some out-crop of rock enchanted me, while another saw me turn away from it, for no other reason than love or enmity. Just as my relationships with humans so frequently left me unmoved, so the feelings I experienced at night proved rich in the extreme, and full of subtle nuances; some tree or other pleased me, some branch which I pulled towards me with the tip of my bayonet seemed brotherly, some leaf made me want to press it against my eyes, some jumble of tall rocks which had fallen from the cliff filled me with alarm. The weight of the hills; the water sparkling in places as it threaded on downstream, straining to carry away dead wood; the moon's dazzling light; even the contours of the land-scape: all of these things I felt as forces, some dangerous, some not. Memories of human settlements, fragments of the Past lived on in the depths of the greenery, in the crevices of the rock; and new forces too, disturbing forces of love and dreams.

I was pushing aside a leaf with the underside of my blade when a young tree with healthy, shining bark appeared before me in all its beauty. It soared quite high into the sky and I loved it instantly. I pressed my cheek against it. I loved it with love. In the darkness, femininity overcame masculinity within me, because I had wanted to visit the place of springs and spells, and so betray mankind in the time of the night.

On my knees at the foot of the tree, pressing my lips to its soft bark, I spoke to it tenderly in a kind of half-sung whisper, drawn from the deepest part of my being and my truth. My song was a little hoarse, modulated in my mouth like an animal's growl. I unfastened my belt buckle, put my arms round the tree and acted the woman with it, my chest bare, my loins bare, gripping the trunk tightly between my thighs. Like this, I sank into pure, simple, absolute, delicious sensual pleasure. I loved the tree, I desired the tree. My personality inclined me to be unreservedly happy. In this land of painted caves, the most distant realms of the Past looked upon me with approval. In my relations with the tree, the womanly part of me derived from the first nights of the earth; this love of leaves dated from the very first evenings, the first Paradises, and gave me the curious character of an enchantress. A deep-seated memory returned to me in a flood of pleasure.

Once I was sated, my masculinity returned to me, and I paid more heed to the beautiful, starry sky. I wanted to see it at closer hand; so I buckled up my belt and climbed into the tree, scaling it from branch to branch, until my head was above its crown. Night was moving on. Many stars were sinking below the horizon. Everything seemed dark and dangerous, except the sky, except the river which spread a blaze of light all around. The hills of the Sarladais, recently so bright and shining, were now covered in mist. Once again I was feeling the cold, so much so that the only desire I now felt was to return as quickly as possible to my bed.

Once I had climbed down from the tree it was impossible to find the path I had taken. The mist had occupied all the low ground, and the sinking moon no longer provided any light. The Vézère was flowing towards the village; since I could not go back the way I came, it seemed to me that the best thing was to float like a piece of dead wood and thus return to the land of the living.

I slid into the water and was surprised to find it almost hot compared to the coldness of the air. I rid myself of my clothes, which I attached firmly to a piece of dry wood with my belt; slipping my bayonet through it, I walked on along the pebbles until I lost my footing and began to swim. The Vézère's powerful current was carrying along branches and leaves, and various kinds of dross. I would have felt fear if my bundle had not supported me so well. The river was giving me respite from living, it was carrying me back to the land of men. Springs murmured, birds sang, I drifted.

Fish leapt and fell back heavily into the silent, dead parts of the river, the deepest parts, where the Vézère became so calm that it seemed motionless. I imagined that I was just a sort of rat, swimming with the current. A smell of decomposition was coming from the muddy banks, planted with dark clumps of trees.

Milky-white mist drifted across the surface of the river. Birds' humble gazes followed me; the sound of beating wings accompanied my journey, and, here and there, cries, squabbles. Pushed along by the current, with no need to swim, I moved among the shadows. Ten metres of water were moving downstream beneath me, carrying me towards my bed. I held my breath, I lived only faintly, I was nothing but a pair of eyes, among those of the birds, in the peaceful night.

My feet met the solid ground of an island. I stretched

out in the grass which grew there among white pebbles covered with a fine film of grey mud, now dry and cracked, which the floods had brought there; and I rested. It was a low-lying island, which the shining, round moon lit up with its glow. Here and there, sand-banks broke the surface of the Vézère, whose waters boiled and sang.

I turned my gaze downstream. There was a gap in the trees, revealing three tall rocks crowned with bushes, towering more than twenty metres above the river's course; they had stood there forever, since the beginning of the Earth and of Man; among the green leaves, before the stars, they were beautiful, like immense patches of whiteness; they looked just like large pieces of fabric, dry-ing in the moonlight. I closed my eyes, opened them again, still astonished to see so much calm splendour.

As I lay on the stones of the island a soft light touched my bayonet and my wet bundle, which lay next to me. I got into the water, seeking sensual pleasure; I found it among the cool flowers which floated on a sort of marsh. I washed myself in the river, no longer sure if I was Man, or Woman, or Nymph.

A sandbar, which stretched across the current, forced me to paddle about among the wild grasses, stirred by the passage of the water like long skeins of green silk spread out on the round, smooth stones, where I lost my footing and scrambled back to my feet. I walked, then threw myself back into the Vézère and it carried me off in its tides with my bundle, which danced on the waves, my bundle which I clung to tightly; and swiftly, very swiftly, the river drew me on towards my bed.

TREMBLING WITH FEVER and cold, I got into bed. Once I was between the sheets my strength of character quickly asserted itself over my tiredness and after a little warmth and rest I was soon myself again. It must have been around three in the morning. My priest did not seem to have returned and I was not displeased to find myself alone. No desire for sleep closed my eyes; on the contrary, the desire to take up pen and ink kept me awake. Delighted, worn-out, home again, I could think of nothing but writing.

The night air touched the flame of my little candle but it scarcely quivered. Exquisite moments at the end of the night. Not a breath of wind. You can see nothing of the World. It is an absence of everything; the seconds are no longer composed of anything; everything seems suspended. The motionless air doesn't shake a single branch; not one bird sings. All you can feel is the intense, all-pervading spell of the supreme life of earth and sky, so powerfully, that all you have to do is dip into it to draw out what you want. From my bedroom, with the window open, I could only discern the nearness of our trees from faint scents of sap, and the presence of the vast Sarladais from other scents carried by the river, whose whisperings I could hear.

My candle spread a halo of calm light, soft and golden.

I watched, and saw myself as being like that little flame, whose glow stood in stubborn opposition to the tranquil shadows.

Is a book born when the idea you already have of it drives away sleep? My solitude and that mad side of me which came from my errant ways presaged nothing good. Knowing myself as I did, I was expecting nothing but the worst. I had read few books, and always at top speed; I was keenly aware that my knowledge of French was rather poor; I spoke it as I heard it, according to sound, hearsay, music, without spelling and without grammar. I lived beside the springs and the woods, with just enough learning to write humbly; this did not give me much hope of creating a work I could feel vain about, which could give a reader pleasure and gain his attention.

In my head, old sentences drawn from old books were mixed up with village expressions, curious provincial turns of phrase, the artless candour of common folk. A tissue of weaknesses run through with follies and naïvety, that was the sort of book I could be the author of.

Despite the keenness of my joy and the possibility that I might wrest it from oblivion, my ability to achieve it seemed to me to be particularly feeble. My isolation plunged me into despair. Can you imagine that: extreme solitude? The only people who had shown me friendship were beings as lost as myself, a priest and a child, and what a priest! It was enough to make me believe that this most ancient land of ghosts and fairies was holding me prisoner; that so much happiness must be paid for with a degree of loneliness which I would have accepted, were I not afraid that I might see what I had to say perish along with myself.

From this perspective I suddenly saw nothing but enemies: myself, with this worrying lack of learning, and other, pitiless men. And what could I hope for, what hope was there, for what unknown solitude? Not a hand to help me, nothing but black, sad silence. I even saw myself as odious, too far removed from other men ever to unite with them.

Then a gleam of light sprang out of that dark night. I told myself that old sentences, from the times of the kings, run through with rustic artlessness, together with my skilfully-woven madness, might weave an astonishing kind of fabric, worthy of survival. A little book, well and badly written at the same time, that is what I might be capable of. A sort of tapestry. It came to me to weave it in coarse wool mixed with fine silk. This idea of a book worked in the manner of a curiously woven fabric pleased me. My solitude immediately seemed interesting to me, my vices too. I could visualise my project clearly, and planned to accomplish it as quickly as possible; I was already entertaining myself with the mischiefs and tricks I intended to cram into this text, which would be made up of a thousand ruses and little weaknesses. I would endow it with all my pleasure in living, the love which burned in my heart, my true nature, and my soul, and the tireless river, and my priest, and the child. Before even beginning it I could already see it, for the idea precedes everything, the rest is only attentive patience, weaving, a game of shuttles; for it is the man of the night who invents, the man of the morning is nothing but a scribe.

I now positively welcomed my solitude. I loved this state of abandonment in which I had been left, loved it as if it were the best part of my being, the most real, the most emotional. Silence no longer terrified me. Once again I sensed that the World was there, next to me, like an intact reserve of delicious forces which I had only to dip into to write a book unlike any other. But what a strange book this would be, created in this way, by a boy like me who lived in a priest's house! A *galant*, almost magical little book, one whose like no one else would ever write. This unique opportunity exhilarated me in the great silence and the darkness, not so much of the sleeping countryside but of my life, so poor and lonely. Whole sentences came to my lips, sleep took hold of me; I closed my eyes tightly in the warmth of my bed as I listened to my own voice for the first time, my voice which sounded as if it were lost in the woods, but more human than so many other voices less humble than mine.

ALL THE SAME, I did not forget the child, nor my soul, hidden in the spring. I placed a stone outside the door of the church, as a signal that I was alone, and entered. The spiral staircase hewn into the wall, and feebly lit every ten steps by narrow loopholes, curved upwards towards immense beams. These were arranged in such a way that they intersected each other and seemed almost infinite in number under the semi-darkened, haunted stone roof onto which rain was falling. After once again exploring this little nook which seemed just right for us, I was about to go back down when I glanced out of the topmost spyhole on the stairs, and saw the child climbing the church steps.

He was well-proportioned, bold, with a laughing face and a hint of flame in his eyes. He stepped lightly, as if he were walking on the tips of his toes. He looked like an angel; quite simply he was my friend, and I loved him. I was exhilarated by the idea that my image would appear in his mind; that in the very same moment he both would hope to see me, and be noticed by me. He entered the courtyard, saw the stone, walked on a little further and disappeared from view. I went down the stairs a little way to try and see him again through a better-placed slit. I was more in love with him than ever.

Not a sound echoed from the church flagstones, nor from the over-narrow, winding staircase. Yet I was sure he was very close by, because of the extraordinary feelings of excitement which flooded into me. Yes, I heard the sound of a light footfall; then silence. More footsteps on the stairs. Then nothing more. And then, as calm and natural as ever, he appeared in front of me and took my hand.

"I have come back," he said.

The rain had plastered his hair to his forehead. I kissed his face. He only appeared calm; his little heart was beating fit to burst. He spoke again: I love you. His embrace was gentle and strong. He was the living, divine incarnation of a spirit full of friendship and courage. Everything conspired with us, places, circumstances; I shall remember my whole life that I saw this, I thought, that this existed; and the face which I loved, which loved me, engraved itself deep in my heart. Standing within the staircase's inconvenient spiral, one shoulder pressed against the cold stone, I held him tightly in my arms. A gentle heat rose from his wet clothes, from his throat, glimpsed through his open-necked, short-sleeved shirt. He had the magical charm of France, of a very ancient France. I had seduced the being most worthy of inspiring love. As usual, there was scented pomade on his hair.

"You must go."

"We have won now, you know," he told me.

He turned his beautiful face towards me. He had learned to kiss; I have never known more tender, more passionate kisses than his; he gave me his brand-new, virgin lips; he was doing this for the first time and putting all his heart into it. When he had gone I stayed on the staircase, leaning against the stone, in the same place where he had tenderly pulled away from my arms. Some of his strength remained on my face, some of his magic; my heart was still beating to the rhythm of love; it would take me several hours to pull myself together, to be myself again.

I did not light a fire, I dared not eat. I filled a big cauldron with soup and went up to my room. It was raining. In bed, I spent the day pleasantly, with his sweet smell still on my face. All I had to do was close my eyes to bring the most delightful memories to life, and to hear his voice telling me: We have won now, you know. I stayed there all afternoon, nice and warm under my blankets, listening to the sound of the rain, breathing in the smell of the leaves, leaning out of bed to drink soup from a ladle, reading fairy stories. The smell of damp tobacco leaves which impregnated the house made me mildly drunk; the far-off storm thundered dully. It remained both close and distant, unwilling to leave us.

Evening came. When my priest arrived, the stern look on his face warned me that it was not good news.

"I don't know if you realise the danger you are running in seeing the child again," he said. "He will talk. I am afraid for you; come, I can save you from the vengeance of men, but you must die. For one single night you must disappear from the number of the living and pass over to our side."

I saw the desire to kill me cross his eyes. Killing for pleasure, if he killed someone it would be me. Strange night. He took oars and disappeared in the direction of the river, swollen by the rain of the last few days. Should I follow him on to the dark Vézère, which growled beneath the branches? A powerful, swift current ran downstream. Our boat was tied up and thudding dully against the river bank. He waded into the turbulent waters; throwing the chain into the bottom of the boat, he strained to push it into the current, which threatened to capsize it immediately, and flung it back violently under the low branches of the trees where it remained stuck fast. "Come," he shouted to me, seizing my hand firmly. We climbed into that heavy boat, which I pushed away from the bank with a shove of my oar. He had run to the river which would decide my fate; for I more or less understood this: knowing we were guilty, though not quite knowing what of, he wanted to lead me to death, with the subconscious thought that we would be absolved of our sins if we emerged from this trial alive; indeed, he ran the risk of drowning along with me, which made him innocent of this murder. It would be the river's judgement, God's perhaps, a trial by ordeal, which corresponded well with his mentality, his habit of deciding nothing for himself.

My memory of travelling down that river is as much one of terror as delight, and also, in a way, almost no memory at all, for I was travelling into the realm of my soul and the realm of death. As soon as we were some distance from the bank, the current took hold of the boat which rolled, spun round on itself, danced on short, choppy waves, and almost threw us into the water; although I was kneeling on the bottom of the boat, I strained to hold it in a straight line with the aid of an oar. The Vézère in flood, whipping our boat, proved to be more than dangerous because of the stones and the sandbanks on which we could have foundered. Deep undercurrents lifted up the bows of our boat, which fell back heavily into the water; brisk, slightly lukewarm air hit our faces; we were carried away without being able to do much to direct our course, or grab hold of a branch, since the speed and weight of the boat tore it out of our hands. At any moment, we could be blinded by the trees under which we passed, unseeing.

The strength of the current, although still considerable, seemed to me to be abating. We were travelling less swiftly on the invisibly lapping waves. The river was growing calmer. I laid the oar across the boat and let it run with the flow of the water. Soon there was silence and a sort of stillness. We drifted gently into the blackness, only light lapping disturbing our slow movement through the shadows, in deep water, under tall cliffs which jutted out to form a vault above our heads. It was so difficult to see anything that we needed a lantern. On the prow, he positioned a helmet from the 1914 war, peppered with holes driven through with a hammer; he filled it with twigs and charcoal which he took from his pockets, and lit it, not without difficulty. And so we continued to sail slowly on; red-hot twigs fell into the water and sizzled for a moment; the holes aerated the helmet quite well, and a bright red blaze, the colour of our burning coals, flamed powerfully around us.

The flames guttered, then almost went out. The moon rose in a beautiful night sky decked with white, transparent clouds; our helmet, balanced on the pointed prow of our boat, gave off only a humble blue smoke, which floated on the Vézère like a train of mist. A small shudder, a bump; the boat turned its nose slowly downstream, and stayed in the middle of the river, while leaves which floated here and there overtook us little by little. Amid the shadows of the night, in low voices, we discussed our situation. A long pole, thrust into the water, did not touch the bottom. A spring which sang under the rocks emptied into the Vézère. Probably we had foundered on the tip of some block of stone or other which had fallen from the cliff and was just below the surface of the water. My priest lowered himself into the river; with a heave of his shoulder he dislodged our wicked boat; then I saw the line of ridges moving across the sky; we had been taken up again by the current. He swam after me. The mass of water began to tremble, announcing the approach of new rapids; I thought it wise to give him a rope, and he tied it around a tree-trunk which our boat had just come alongside. We climbed out; pushing aside the leaves, groping our way, we searched for a shelter against the cold of the night. Our hands encountered dry wood, we lit a fire without really knowing what instinct had led us there in the half-darkness.

Our flames revealed a vast cave, a chamber even, hewn into the rock, where you could sleep on a sort of platform if you climbed up to it; there were planks there, an extraordinarily dry, powdery earth floor, a real fireplace, stacks of firewood. In front of the fire we stacked up our possessions to form a kind of bed, made up of clothes and blankets which we had brought out with us. The surroundings were quite damp and it would have been rather cold in the realm of the dead if we had not fuelled our fire with fresh wood; he plunged into the depths of the undergrowth; working hard and without respite, he pulled tangled trees towards himself, long branches which he threw at my legs, quickly supplying me with a pile of dry wood which the rocky overhang had protected from the rain.

With an immense crackling sound and bright flashes of flame, our inferno cast a powerful brilliance over one whole side of the river. He remained standing in front of the fire, a blanket draped over his shoulders, his legs spattered with earth and leaves, saying nothing, deep in thought. He took his knife, cut a deep slash in his wrist and threw blood on to the firewood, which our flames were devouring. We were, to say the least, beyond customary reality, in an altered state whose danger I knew only too well; for I was with a being who was highly unstable, and whose kind of love for me could end very badly. The invincible need to destroy me hardened his face. He glared stubbornly into the fire, his blanket on his shoulders, wrapping part of the front around his legs and his blood-blackened hand. He was thinking about me, I had no doubt about that.

"You must undergo the same," he told me after a long silence, showing me a long scar in the the thickest part of his calf, a furrow ploughed by a blade heated on burning coals.

I accepted enthusiastically. Yelling with pain as the fire burned me would bring me happiness. Renewing the secret agreement which bound us together would protect me from prison.

"A blade heated on burning brands," he continued, laying the knife on the embers.

So much heat was coming off our flames that they were drying out the bushes all around and burning our faces and hands. Our shadows danced. In that cave, he lay down on a piece of scarlet fabric from Africa or Oceania. I rolled him cigarettes while sleep took hold of us, perhaps caused by the fierce heat from the inferno, or by the sound of the water flowing by; wind blew in off the river, fanning the flames. I was beyond fear, beyond myself; maddened by the murmur of the water, by the idea of death, I remembered that I had already lived, that I was no more than a spirit. Laughing at my fears, like a dreaming god, I felt an all-conquering gaiety. Gnawed away by the flames, our pile of firewood collapsed. He would have burned me with the point of his knife, if the delicious peace of the night had not suddenly plunged us into a half-sleep. Many feelings troubled my soul, feelings moreover that were exquisitely sweet, for fear had left me now. Among them was gratitude for this man who had brought me into this land of shadows in order to save me.

My eyes had been closed for a long time when, opening them again, I saw that our fire was dying down and the moon hung low in the sky. Moonglow lit up the Vézère as it passed beneath the trees, its waters forming a riot of small, noisy waves as it flowed over stones close to an island. Millions of mayflies with diaphanous wings were flying back upstream, against the current; you might have thought it was a mist, a migration of souls. I did not move from underneath my blankets, and only my gaze was carried towards the riverbank, turned white by the wedding flight of the mayflies.

My priest was sleeping next to me. Did I dream in the darkness as it was pierced by great rays of moonlight? It would be easy to imagine the whole thing was nothing but a dream. Our burned-up trees were no more than cinders among the green grass from which a thin grey smoke rose; all that was left of them now was a tracery of their former selves on the ground, dotted here and there with scarlet sparks. And so the judgement of the river had spared us; but I must give up the child; a sort of voice told me so clearly; I must lose him, now, tonight, until another life.

Getting up, pushing away my blankets, I picked up my short iron sword and threw it far away from me, with the thought that it was my love for the child which I was burying under ten metres of water, in the darkest part of the Vézère's bed where no one would ever find it. That done, I swam silently into the zones of calm and light, into the peace of the night under the overhanging cliffs, hollowed by erosion, haunted by the water's murmur. The memory of my drowned love pierced my heart like a sweet blade of flame; I wished I could roll down like a stone to join it and hold it in my arms, at the very depths of death; I wished I could die, yet all the time the same little voice kept stubbornly repeating: in another life, in another life, you will find me again.

My priest was waiting for me on the bank, still holding his blanket tightly around him. When we got back to the cave, he stoked up the embers, and when we had warmed up a little, I saw him flatten down a heap of hot cinders with his bloody hand, and in it draw squares which he filled with pebbles. Did he wish to tell my horoscope? Would I go to prison? That was what tormented me. I asked him to see my future. I will try, he said. He took one of the pebbles, closed his eyes, threw it onto the cinders; then another; several pebbles had landed on the squares. He examined their positions, considered, then threw some of them again to see the future more clearly.

"I see a trial, judges, police."

He thought again, as though confused by a doubt. He rubbed everything out, and began to redraw the squares, and throw the pebbles again.

"It's incredible. I see the child, the trial, the judges; I see all that business. The child will talk without throwing too much of the blame on you, as much from some vestige of love for you, as through caution; I see an acquittal, you needn't worry about that; but what I can't see, not at all, is you."

I asked him if he often told horoscopes.

"From time to time," he replied, as though I were insinuating that he knew nothing of the craft. "I've never seen a case like it: the absence of someone who is not dead, who goes up before the judges, and yet who isn't there."

He threw other stones on to the squares, one last time, to put his mind at rest, carefully examined the positions, then wiped everything away furiously.

"You are not dead, it is as if you are absent from your own trial."

A gleam entered my eyes.

"If I wasn't absent from my trial, like you say, would I be found guilty?"

"Of course, your guilt is clear."

"Then where am I?"

I took his hand:

"Where am I, now?"

He pulled out a hair, attached a small stone to it, drew a rough map of the area in the ashes of the fire, and moved the pendulum over it.

"We are here on the Vézère."

"No, you are here on the Vézère, but not me; look, I'm somewhere else, go back up the Vézère."

The pendulum came to a halt a long way upstream from the village.

"I see a spring," he said, "and I see you."

"That's where I hid my soul."

"There, in the spring?"

"Yes."

"You are strong," he murmured. Then he added: "You will have to take it back after your trial; don't forget."

"Do you really think I would forget my soul," I said, leaning affectionately against him.

He stood up. We rolled our blankets into a bundle, stamped out the last embers, crossed the river in our boat and, after a long walk through the woods, we arrived back at the presbytery.

It was three o'clock in the morning; perhaps we were drunk with exhaustion? Nevertheless, before going up to bed we decided on a celebration. In the kitchen he gave me a little bread, and some wine. There was a long silence, then I poured him a drink. "There you are," I said. He drank without answering, but I thought I saw a smile on his lips, a smile formed from great friendship. "To your good health," he replied, and I saw clearly that what he meant was the happy outcome of my trial. I would willingly have raised my glass in honour of the magic which had protected me so well. And in my heart I heard the child's softly-whispered words: "We have won now, you know".

AFTERWORD

FRANÇOIS AUGIÉRAS was born on 18 July 1925, at Rochester in New York State; his father, a pianist and music teacher working in the United States, had just died from peritonitis. In November, mother and child began their return journey to Paris, setting sail on the *France* with the dead man's embalmed body in the ship's hold.

Augiéras spent his early childhood in Paris, but left at eight to live in Périgueux—the Dordogne was to become his base and his refuge in a life fragmented by journeys and escapes. At thirteen, he left school to learn drawing. For a while he belonged to the *Jeunesse de France et d'Outre-mer*, then in 1943 he joined the *Compagnons de France*, an organisation allied to the scouting movement. Whilst with them, he supervised delinquent children and worked on farms. In the summer of 1944, with the agreement of the Périgueux branch of the *Forces Françaises de l'Intérieur* (the French Resistance) he left the town for Toulon. There, he signed on at the 5th depot of the *Équipages de la Flotte* and travelled to Camp Sirocco in Algiers. Invalided out, he remained in Algeria for about a year, staying first in a Trappist monastery at Thibar, then in a *bordj* (fort) at El Goléa with an uncle who was a retired colonel—the ancestral, mystagogical figure of this man was to play a major role in Augiéras's work and imagination. On his return to Périgord, he became involved with a small group of people interested in art and painting, explored the region on foot, visited the islands of the Vézère, and slept in abandoned farms, far from a "degraded civilisation".

The first work by this pantheistic, pagan mystic, *Le Vieillard et l'Enfant* (*The Old Man and the Child*) appeared in 1949. It was published by Pierre Fanlac, at the author's expense, under the pseudonym of Abdullah Chaanba (Chaamba in later editions). This tale of an intensely private, erotic and spiritual education in the Sahara enchanted Gide, who wrote to him: "Whom have I to thank for this intense and bizarre delight?" In 1954, the unabridged version of *Le Vieillard et l'Enfant*, published by Éditions de Minuit, revived the question raised by the author of *Les nourritures terrestres*: who was Abdullah Chaamba?

Augiéras loved mystery. Elusive and secretive, forever penniless, this anti-Christian nomad travelled constantly: Delphi, Mount Athos, Senegal, Mauritania. During this time Frédérick Tristan's *Structure* published several examples of Augiéras's writing. In 1958, he spent a few months as a member of the Saharan police, defending the fort at Zirara. The following year, he worked in Mali as an ethnographer, and published his second book, *Voyage des Morts* (*Voyage of the Dead*), again under the name of Chaamba. He married a distant cousin, Viviane de la Ville de Rigné and lived with his wife in Périgueux. When he was not writing, he produced abstract or realist paintings. In the Sixties, he began work on a volume of memoirs; this book, *Une adolescence au Temps du Maréchal et de multiples Aventures* (*The Many Adventures of an Adolescent Boy in the Age of the Marshal*), published in 1967, was the first under the name of Augiéras. He was often to be found at the community of *l'Arche Lanza Del Vasto*, in Hérault. He spent more and more time with the Orthodox monks of Mount Athos—his retreats inspired him in 1970 to write *Un voyage au Mont Athos* (*A Journey to Mount Athos*—1970), which dealt in particular with reincarnation and physical pleasure as a means of purifying the soul. But his health was in decline and a heart attack forced him to move into a residential home at Domme, in the Dordogne, where he eventually lived, meditated and worked in a cave. There, cocooned in a primeval, silent world, he wrote *Domme ou l'Essai d'Occupation* (*Domme, or An Attempt at Occupation*)—this book did not find a publisher until eleven years after his death. Although in 1970 and 1971 he was an inmate of the hospice at Montignac, he continued to travel to Greece, and to Tunis, where he exhibited his work.

This man, whom his friend Paul Placet* saw as "a barbarian in the West", this man who lived bare-legged, with his head in the stars, died in hospital at Périgueux on 13 February 1971, from the after-effects of a heart attack. He was forty-five years old.

L'Apprenti Sorcier (*The Sorcerer's Apprentice*) belongs to French literature's pantheon of secret, underground texts. The story was first published in 1964, at the writer, Jacques Brenner's instigation. It appeared anonymously in *Les Cahiers des Saisons* (Éditions Julliard), and the only clue given was that it was "by the author of *Le Vieillard et l'Enfant*".

In the depths of Black Périgord, in the Sarladais, "a land of ghosts, cool caves and woods", a teenage boy is sent to live with a thirty-five-year-old priest. The man will become more than just a teacher. Soon, the adolescent meets a young boy in the village square: they make love to each other like shadows in a cave. The priest knows of their involvement; far from condemning it, he intensifies it. He teaches his pupil about pain and the whip, awakening his senses to exquisitely pleasurable mortification and guiding him to seek out his own soul. The adolescent ceases to be a mere pupil and becomes first a servant, then an initiate. Soon he

*For observations on Augiéras's life, personality, writings and paintings, see his work, *François Augiéras: Un barbare en Occident*, Pierre Fanlac, 1988.

will be able to detect "with an extreme intensity, the secret movements of life, the growth of plants, the fermentation of stagnant waters, here an imperceptible movement of air, there the crack of a branch". He will hide his soul, sheltering it from men, in a secret spring of the Vézère; he will triumph against the laws of society. And it becomes clear that this tense, shadowy tale, burning with love, is a eulogy in praise of difference, an apprenticeship to purity, an act of worship to beauty in the temple of *Périgordin* nature.

The facts are simple, naked and brutal, but what takes place between the three characters of this mystical ballet—characters who are pure essences, rather than rounded individuals, and who are described in very little detail—comes close to being supernatural. Augiéras knew this, mentioning at the turn of a page that he wished to create: "A *galant*, almost magical book", "an astonishing piece of fabric which deserves to survive". It has survived.

Cahiers rouges, Grasset, 1995

Sketch for a Systematic Metaphysics

David Armstrong sets out his metaphysical system in a set of concise and lively chapters each dealing with one aspect of the world. He begins with the assumption that all that exists is the physical world of space-time. On this foundation he constructs a coherent metaphysical scheme that gives plausible answers to many of the great problems of metaphysics. He gives accounts of properties, relations, and particulars; laws of nature; modality; abstract objects such as numbers; and time and mind.

David Armstrong was Challis Professor of Philosophy at the University of Sydney until his retirement in 1992.

Sketch for a Systematic Metaphysics

D.M. Armstrong

CLARENDON PRESS · OXFORD

OXFORD
UNIVERSITY PRESS

Great Clarendon Street, Oxford OX2 6DP
United Kingdom

Oxford University Press is a department of the University of Oxford.
It furthers the University's objective of excellence in research, scholarship,
and education by publishing worldwide. Oxford is a registered trade mark of
Oxford University Press in the UK and in certain other countries

British Library Cataloguing in Publication Data

Data available

Library of Congress Cataloging in Publication Data

Data available

ISBN 978-0-19-959061-2 (Hbk)
ISBN 978-0-19-965591-5 (Pbk)

Printed in the United Kingdom by
Lightning Source UK Ltd., Milton Keynes

For Jenny

Contents

Preface

In 2008 I was asked to give a course in metaphysics at the Graduate Center of the City University of New York (CUNY). I was uncertain what to base the course on. I had previously, in 2005, given a course there based on my book *Truth and Truthmakers* (Armstrong 2004) and it seemed that I should not repeat that. But what should I substitute? The following idea came to me. The years when analytic philosophy was dominated first by the ideas of the logical positivists and then by the 'ordinary language' approach that became fashionable in Oxford were thankfully long gone. Gone also were the objections that were made to traditional metaphysics by these philosophers. Metaphysics is now respectable again. But, it seems, metaphysics, though pursued by many very talented philosophers, is at present done in a rather piecemeal way. It is rare to find a systematic approach to the subject. But, I thought, I do have something that may be called a metaphysical system. Why should I not present it to my seminar?

A text I wrote out for the CUNY lectures served as a first draft for this not very long sketch of my metaphysics. I did present my system some years ago in *A World of States of Affairs* (Armstrong 1997a). More recently Stephen Mumford published a book *David Armstrong* in a series Philosophy Now, which I think is excellent (Mumford 2007). It does not confine itself to my metaphysics, though metaphysics gets the most space.

My views, however, though their general direction is the same, have been revised in certain places. In particular, it is only relatively recently that I have realized just how important is the notion of a *truthmaker* for tying up many issues. Again, I have, after a good deal of chopping and changing, reached a new view of the 'fundamental tie' between particulars and universals. The 1997 book, furthermore, was very much a work for professionals. I found that I wanted to write something deliberately directed towards students, graduate students, and even undergraduates, and perhaps even towards the general educated reader with an interest in philosophy. So some things are explained here which the working philosopher will not need to have explained.

We learn by teaching, as a Latin proverb has it, and, not surprisingly, the explaining I do in this sketch has in turn helped to modify some of my views a little further. At the same time, I have given all the references that are required by academic convention, including introducing some footnotes that, however, may be safely skipped.

I'd like to emphasize, cannot indeed overemphasize, the tentative nature of what I present here. Philosophers may not like to admit it, but fashion is an important factor in philosophy. And once fashion comes in, objectivity goes. The reason is rather obvious: philosophy lacks the wonderful *decision procedures* that are present in logic and mathematics (proofs) and the natural sciences (observation and experiment, together with mathematics). Unfortunately there seems to be no remedy for this situation, and those who thought there is a remedy, such as the logical positivists, learnt bitter lessons. But since this is so, we philosophers should be appropriately modest.

I've adopted a reasonably colloquial style, as though these are lectures. My own introduction to metaphysics was through attending dictated lectures by John Anderson during 1949 and 1950, then Challis Professor of Philosophy at the University of Sydney. The subject was said to be the book *Space, Time and Deity* by Samuel Alexander, being the Gifford Lectures given at Glasgow, 1916–1918. Anderson had heard these lectures while a student at Glasgow University, and, while a senior student, had discussions with the affable Alexander.[1] Anderson took a few leading ideas from Alexander, but primarily the objective was to present, via criticism of Alexander, Anderson's own metaphysics. These lectures have been salvaged and put together as a book, edited by Creagh Cole with an Introduction by myself: *Space, Time and the Categories* (2007). Anderson's scheme of metaphysical categories, where he followed in a tradition set by Plato, Aristotle, Kant, Hegel, and Samuel Alexander, is of some interest, I think.

Two other persons had a major influence on my thinking about metaphysics. One was C.B. (Charlie) Martin who introduced me to the all-important notion of a truthmaker. A second was David Lewis. Lewis and I had many disagreements about metaphysics. I do not accept his view that all the possible worlds really exist. I reject his account of laws of nature as mere regularities in the world, and also his account of causality in terms of counterfactuals – that is, in terms of what would have happened in the absence of the cause. But again and again discussions with him were fruitful, even where we disagreed, and he taught me much. James Franklin,

[1] For an interesting life of John Anderson see *A Passion to Oppose*, by Brian Kennedy, a historian.

Anne Newstead, and I have worked together recently, our aim being to produce elements of an 'Aristotelian' philosophy of mathematics, work reflected in this book. Jacob Berger and Dan Shargel made excellent contributions to the 2008 seminars, contributions acknowledged in the text. Jim Durham, Bob Fry, and Joan Symington are not philosophers but do have an educated interest in the subject. I thank them for reading the manuscript and giving me valuable comments. Noa Latham and Gonzalo Rodriguez-Pereyra also read the text and made very helpful suggestions.

There are 16 chapters, which may seem an excessive number for a short work. But philosophy is often best digested if you take small bites.

Chapter 1

Introduction

I begin with the assumption that all that exists is the space-time world, the physical world as we say. What argument is offered for this assumption? All I can say is that this is a position that many – philosophers and others – would accept. Think of it this way. This is a *hypothesis* that many would accept as plausible. The space-time entity seems obviously to exist. Other suggested beings seem much more hypothetical. So let us start from this position and see if a coherent metaphysical scheme, one that gives a plausible answer to many of the great problems of metaphysics, can be erected on this relatively narrow foundation. After all, it is folly to think that, by philosophical reasoning, one can *prove* that any particular scheme of ontology (another term for metaphysics, but one that tends to concentrate on the general nature of things) is correct. What we can hope for is a vision (hopefully coherent) of the fundamental structure of the world, a vision that will then compete with other visions. I argue where I can, but at times I simply assert.

The restriction of what there is to space-time means the rejection of what many contemporary philosophers call 'abstract objects', meaning such things as numbers or the Platonic Forms or classes, where these are supposed to exist 'outside of' or 'extra to' space-time. The phrase 'abstract

objects' originates with W.V. Quine[1] but it involves a rather extraordinary use of the word 'abstract'. One quite strong argument against these so-called 'abstract entities' is that it is hard to see what *causal role* such beings would play. And if they play no causal role it is hard to see how we can have good reasons for thinking they exist. The thought that the entities we postulate should have causal roles was formalized by Graham Oddie (1982). He christened it the Eleatic Principle.[2] Note that the phrase 'causal roles' allows us to think that different sorts of entity may play different sorts of causal role. But if an entity plays no causal role at all, then that is a good argument, though perhaps not a conclusive one, for not postulating that entity.

I say that I restrict being, what exists, to the space-time world. This is by no means to rule out an account of space-time which makes it very different from the relatively simple picture of a single three-dimensional space and an extra dimension of time which has a past, has a present, and advances inexorably into the future. Following the terminology introduced by the US philosopher Wilfrid Sellars we can call this the *manifest image*, the commonsense view, of space-time (Sellars 1968). It was the view held by scientists until the end of the 19th century. It was overthrown by Einstein's Special Relativity theory, which made the present into a relative notion, relative to the inertial system in which observations are made. There followed Einstein's General Relativity theory that introduced the distortion of space by matter, perhaps because matter *was* that distortion. Nowadays, for cosmologists

---

[1] See for instance his essay 'On What There Is' in his book *From a Logical Point of View*, 1961.

[2] After the suggestion of the Eleatic Stranger in Plato's *Sophist* 247D–E. See also Armstrong 1997a, 3.82.

and quantum theorists the nature of space-time, the *scientific image* as Sellars would have said, is up for grabs and in many a theorist's mind it is utterly different from the manifest image. Philosophers, I take it, must just follow the lead of natural science here, and natural science has so far produced no generally agreed-upon theory.

But if we follow the lead of natural science why do we not foreclose any appeal to metaphysics? Why not just hand over the inquiry to science? The answer is that there are a great number of notions that, following the lead of Gilbert Ryle and J.J.C. (Jack) Smart, we can call *topic neutral* notions. Instances are cause, class, property, relation, quality, kind, resemblance, quantity, number, substance, fact, truth, law of nature, power, and others. These notions are perfectly general, are very difficult to analyse and interconnect, and give rise to controversy, sometimes to bitter controversy, when we (and the 'we' here includes scientists as much as philosophers) try to discuss them. They are not exhausted by logic or mathematics. It is these sorts of notions, I suggest, that metaphysics strives to give a systematic account of.

Let us take the topic of causation as an example. What is causation? Beyond the judgements of causation that ordinary life furnishes us with, pushing that cup caused it to fall and break, we look to empirical science to tell us what causes what. And science has amazingly enlarged our knowledge of what does cause what. Science has taught us that laws of nature in general take a mathematical form and, much more recently, that the data seem to show that the laws are probabilistic only, a difficult idea, and something we would not have come to naturally. But what do philosophers say causation is? Here are some, *only some*, of the views. Some see it as no more than regularity in the way things happen,

echoing what may have been David Hume's view. But others think that it is a *making* things happen in the individual sequence, this bullet causing this death, with any regularities a secondary matter. David Lewis held that causality was a connection of events subject to the truth of a *counterfactual*: if the first event, the cause, had not occurred then neither would the second event, the effect, have occurred. Others hold that causings are manifestations of powers, where the powers *necessitate* the manifestation. Phil Dowe partly turns back to science, arguing that causality is the possession of a *conserved quantity* in interactions that makes a process a causal process (Dowe 2000). Philosophical analyses of causation, as you see from this selection, a selection only, can be widely different. Now surely this matter ought to be debated, and it is debated. It is a *philosophical* debate about the nature of causality. Science does not settle the matter, though we have noted that it makes a large contribution. To debate the matter is to engage in metaphysics. The same difficult situation can be reproduced for the other topic neutral notions mentioned above. Agreement about their nature, and how they are interrelated, is very hard to get.

C.B. Martin, in a book published shortly before his death, *The Mind in Nature*, makes the following suggestion:

Ontology sets out an even more abstract model of how the world is than theoretical physics, a model that has *placeholders* for scientific results and *excluders* for tempting confusions. Ontology and theoretical science can help one another along, we hope, with minimal harm.   (Martin 2008, p.42)

Martin's suggestion serves, I think, as a good charter for a metaphysics. Notice that Martin's word 'abstract' bears the traditional, not Quine's, meaning of the word. To abstract is

to concentrate on some feature of things to the exclusion of other features, in Martin's case the most general features of things. That is what we metaphysicians would like to do: to set out such a model for the general features of things. Quine, as noted above, takes an abstract object to be something outside space-time. The hypothesis of this book is that there are no such objects.

Chapter 2
Properties

Let us begin with *properties* of objects, such things as colours, shape, temperature, mass. They will lead us to *states of affairs*: entities that lie at the centre of my ontology. Russell and Wittgenstein called them *facts* and I am simply following in their footsteps with a difference in terminology. See Russell's *The Philosophy of Logical Atomism* (1918) and Wittgenstein's *Tractatus* (1922). Wittgenstein, in my view, was taking a lead from Russell, the greatest metaphysician of the 20th century.

It would seem natural to accept the existence of properties. Things are coloured in particular ways, they have different shapes and sizes, they are hot or cold or in between, they have different weights. Scientific investigation rapidly endorses classifying things by their properties. For instance, it takes the commonsense property of weight and develops the more sophisticated and important property of mass. You weigh less on the moon, but your mass does not change. At a deeper level it postulates the property of rest-mass, the mass a body has when it is at rest as opposed to what it has when it moves. A very large part of empirical science lies in uncovering the properties of things, an uncovering that has had prodigious success.

It is the case, nevertheless, that until rather recently many in the analytic tradition have been inclined to deny the existence of properties in the world, deny the existence of

properties *in re* in the Latin phrase that is often used. This position is traditionally called 'Nominalism', though the word sometimes bears other senses. We should therefore begin by giving this sceptical view some attention. There are various types of Nominalism: Predicate, Class, Resemblance, and what I call 'Ostrich' Nominalism. (See Armstrong 1989 for an introductory book on these issues.) Predicate Nominalists hold that properties are the mere shadows cast by predicates. (See John Searle 1969; he says: 'to put it briefly, universals [so-called] are parasitic on predicate expressions', p.120. Trying to solve metaphysical problems by 'semantic ascent', that is, by appealing to language, was typical of the period.) I hope we can pass this position by. A more interesting view is *Class* Nominalism. To have the property of whiteness is to be a member of the class of white things. This is a 'set-theoretical' treatment of properties. The really interesting question that then arises is whether *every* class of objects constitutes a property, even if it is a property that we have no name for, no use for, and no interest in. That would be a thoroughgoing Class Nominalism, but at the same time it is rather implausible. David Lewis held that view at one time; see his paper 'New Work for a Theory of Universals' (Lewis 1999). The first note of his paper credits me with changing his mind on this matter. He says that otherwise 'I might well have believed to this day that set theory applied to *possibilia* is all the theory of properties that anyone could ever need'.

Lewis speaks of 'possibilia' here instead of 'particulars' as one might expect because he holds that the beings of every possible world exist. In this paper Lewis also calls attention to Quine's equally strange view that to introduce classes is to Platonize (to postulate non-spatiotemporal entities such as Plato's Forms) and so to abandon Nominalism. This is

because Quine thought that classes are 'abstract entities', outside space-time. I see no reason to think that classes are abstract entities, provided their members exist. Then, I think, classes supervene on their members – that is to say, once you are given the members, their class adds nothing ontologically, is no addition of being.[1] So there is no threat from classes to a space-time ontology. But even if classes are 'abstract entities' outside space-time as Quine thought, a class theory of properties is still a Nominalism.

Let us agree, then, that some classes are better than others. We might call the better ones property classes. What analysis will the Class Nominalist give of such classes? One line to take is that the distinction is primitive. Some classes are better than others, and that is all that can be said. (Though the Class theorist would presumably allow distinctions in degree of betterness.) Lewis thought to the end of his life that this sort of Class Nominalism was an option – though he also thought *tropes* (to be discussed shortly) and *universals* were options also. He made no decision about which of the three views to back.

Here is an argument against the first view: that there are property classes, but their goodness is primitive, unanalysable. It is a *Euthyphro* dilemma, of the sort that we find in Plato's dialogue the *Euthyphro*. Does the individual member have the property F (whiteness say) *because* it is a member of the class of white things? Or is it a member of the class in virtue of what it is itself? (The original *Euthyphro* dilemma was: what makes an act a good act? Is it just because it is pleasing to the gods? Or is it pleasing to the gods in virtue of its intrinsically

---

[1] Wade Martin has reminded me about the empty class, which logicians make a member of every class. But I don't accept that this 'class' exists. It would be a strange addition to space-time!

good nature?) I'd suggest that it is very implausible to say that a particular is white in virtue of its membership of the class of white things, but plausible to say that the particular is in this class because of its whiteness. If so, this seems a good reason (not conclusive, but strong) to reject the Class Nominalist view. A second argument is that if there had been more, or less, white things, that is, if the class of white things had contained rather different white particulars, this altered class would seem not to affect their whiteness.

Class theories are extensional – spreading out – theories, and, as a psychological fact, the human mind works better with extensions. For instance, consider the use of possible worlds popularized by David Lewis. Talking of possible worlds takes possibilities extensionally, and they are certainly helpful in thinking about possibility even if you do not believe in the existence of possible worlds. One can 'picture' the different possibilities more easily. Or consider the Venn diagrams, circles used in the traditional logic to picture logical relations between the terms of propositions. They help a lot. The same holds for probabilities (see the very illuminating book by Gerd Gigerenzer 2002). One can 'picture' probabilities much more easily if one takes them as proportions, say out of 100. But the *intensional* view – the opposite of extensionalist theories – in the present case the view that there are properties *in re,* in the world, which determine the extension of the class – is very often, I think, more satisfactory in metaphysics.

A third position a Property Nominalist can embrace is to take resemblance and *degrees of resemblance* holding between particulars as primitives, and then to suggest that the class of white things, say, is constituted by the resemblances that hold between the members of the class. This is not quite an

intensional theory, but it starts to work away from extensional theories. On this view class members are linked to each other by the relation of resemblance which creates a unity in virtue of which the members are said to have 'the same property'. (An *aristocratic* resemblance theory sets up one or more *paradigm* objects to which the other members of the class approximate in resemblance.)

In my opinion this is a superior brand of Property Nominalism. It is the position taken by John Locke, although he did not work out the details very far. But it is exposed to various difficulties. In my book *Nominalism and Realism* (1978a) I assembled all the arguments that have traditionally been advanced against Resemblance Nominalism, thinking that after a recital of these arguments I did not have to bother too much about this theory. How wrong I was! A younger Argentinian philosopher, Gonzalo Rodriguez-Pereyra, set out in his doctoral dissertation at Cambridge to show that the arguments could be met. He largely succeeded. For those familiar with Dan Dennett's delightful *Philosophical Lexicon*, available on the net and full of good philosophy jokes, he 'exhumed' a position previously thought 'humed'. Rodriguez-Pereyra's book (2002) is a wonderful exposition of 'exhuming', although later chapters are very complex. But here are two further objections to his theory. As he says himself, he seems to need a realistic view of possible worlds to answer a difficulty about coextensive properties, that is, properties with the very same extension. How is a resemblance theory to separate them? Furthermore he needs a rather precise theory of resemblances, which for him come in 'units' of resemblance. This is a difficulty, I think, because resemblance in practice seems a messy and inexact notion.

A final Nominalist position that demands consideration is what I call 'Ostrich' Nominalism. See the debate between Michael Devitt and myself. (Both papers are reprinted in the useful Oxford paperback *Properties*, edited by Hugh Mellor and Alex Oliver.) The idea is that one needs no theory of properties at all and so one can ignore the whole dispute. Devitt does not quite embrace this position, but makes it clear that he would like to get rid of 'attributes' (properties).

If one rejects all these views, as I do, we are committed to there being properties. It is a very natural postulate to make. Consider a certain billiard ball. It has a certain mass and it has a certain colour. It may be in motion or at rest on the table. So the metaphysician seems to be on solid ground in postulating objective properties of mass, surface colour, rest, or motion. Truthmaker arguments are quite strong here. These properties all appear to be intrinsic, non-relational. To have nothing but the ball itself being a truthmaker for both 'the ball is red' and 'the ball is spherical', and so on, seems rather implausible. It is certainly very undiscriminating. (A truthmaker is that particular entity in the world in virtue of which a true proposition is true. It is a relatively new version of the *correspondence* theory of truth, and truthmaker theory will figure largely at various points in this book.)

There are further positive arguments that seem to make the case for introducing properties quite strong. Consider the apparently necessary truths:

1. Red resembles orange more than it resembles blue
2. Red is a colour

The first of these examples was put forward by Arthur Pap (1959), the second by Frank Jackson (1977). They appear

to be about properties, and attempts to analyse these truths without mention of properties run into great difficulties.

Thus, consider a suggested paraphrase:

1'. If x is a red particular, and y is an orange particular and z is a blue particular, then x resembles y more than it resembles z.

Proposition 1 is true, but it is easy to find counter-instances to the paraphrase. Let x be a red car and z a blue car of the same make and model. Now let y be a ripe orange. The respects in which x and z resemble far outweigh the respects in which x resembles y. And what are these 'respects' but properties? Again, 2. 'Red is a colour' entails 'for all x, if x is red, it is coloured'. But that entailment seems not strong enough as a *translation*. Jackson points out that the proposition 'for all x, if x is red, x is extended' may equally claim to be a necessary truth. But we don't think that red is an extension.

So it seems that we ought to accept properties into our ontology. But many matters still remain unsettled. A major issue is whether properties should be taken as universals or as particulars ('tropes' in the terminology first used by Donald C. Williams and now popular among philosophers). Consider two billiard balls that have completely indistinguishable colours (both the very same shade of red, let us say). An upholder of universals will urge that there is just one property here – a certain shade of redness. But the trope theorist considers that there are two shades of redness here – properties that are particulars, as particular as the objects that have them. How is the unity of the class of things that are this exact shade of colour to be secured by the trope theorist? It is now generally agreed that this is done by introducing the relation of resemblance. Resemblance has *degrees* together with

a highest degree: exact resemblance. This highest degree is a symmetrical, transitive, and reflexive relation. (A relation is *symmetrical* if when *a* has it to *b*, *b* has it to *a*. It is *transitive* if when *a* has it to *b*, and *b* has it to *c*, then *a* has it to *c*. It is *reflexive* if *a* has it to itself.) Such relations pick out *equivalence classes* that can then be used as a substitute for the *identity* that is postulated by those who accept universals. I lean to properties as universals rather than tropes, but the difference between the power of the two theories is not, I now think, very great. But when we get to *laws of nature* it will be argued that universals have one great advantage over tropes, an advantage that I hope may be decisive.

Notice that the trope view is sometimes, with quite good reason, called 'moderate Nominalism'. It accepts properties, but denies that they are universals. It is a 'middle way' that many metaphysicians uphold.

Another issue that arises for both universals and tropes is that between *attribute* theories and *bundle* theories. Bundle theories, to take them first, are so enamoured of properties that particulars, ordinary things, are held to be bundles of properties. Consider all the properties of a billiard ball. On a bundle view the billiard ball is just all of its properties, bundled together by a relation that is often called *compresence*. You can have bundles of universals: the theory adopted by Russell, though only in his later years. He did not get many followers for this view. Or you can have bundles of tropes – the classic, though not the first 'bundle of tropes' theory, is the great essay by the Harvard philosopher Donald Williams: 'The Elements of Being'. See D.C. Williams 1966.

Bundle theories make properties the only fundamental constituents of particulars. But attribute theorists (I'm among them) hold that there are particulars that *have* the properties.

Properties are attributes of particulars. It is sometimes thought that attribute theorists are saddled with a Lockean substance, in John Locke's words 'something we know not what'. That is not correct at all, I think. We are just as aware, say in perception, of the particularity of things – the 'this' and the 'that' – as we are aware of (some) of the properties of things. We perceive that the ball, a particular, is spherical and red. Particularity, I think, is a fundamental metaphysical category that can't be analysed away *and it is given to us in experience.* Aristotle was an attribute theorist, but shows no sign of thinking that particularity is 'something we know not what'.

You will observe that we have a two by two classification of theories here (bundle vs. attribute, universals vs. tropes) with all four boxes filled by actual eminent philosophers. There is one slight complication: you can accept *both* universals and tropes. The English philosopher John Cook Wilson (1926) is such a case. It seems a bit uneconomical but it can be done. (I'll suggest a reason for holding such a position shortly.)

Going back to property theory we need to make a distinction between non-relational properties and relational properties, though with the object of getting the second sort of property out of the way. This distinction is *not* just the distinction between properties and relations, as the examples that follow show. The shape, the size, and, it would seem, the mass, of objects are non-relational properties of particulars. They are sometimes called the intrinsic properties, though one has to be careful with that word. Examples of relational properties are being five miles from any town, or being taller than the Empire State Building. Relational properties thus involve relations (being five miles from, or being taller than) but are not themselves relations. Our ordinary discourse is full of ascriptions of relational properties, but in this metaphysics

at least, they are much less important because they can be replaced without loss by *relations* between particulars. Suppose that you have all the particulars and all the relations in which these particulars enter into, are not all the relational properties there automatically? In more technical language, the relational properties *supervene*, supervene with necessity, on the properties and the relations. It can be tricky, sometimes, to determine whether a certain property is or is not relational (that is why I was a little hesitant to claim mass as a non-relational property) but if it is relational then it is of less ontological importance as a property because of this supervenience.

Now I will argue for something more controversial, but central to my thinking. I maintain that all properties are *instantiated*. That is to say, a property must be a property of a particular. Properties don't have to be instantiated *now*, past or future is enough. But they must be instantiated somewhere, somewhen. (To accept this is to be an 'omnitemporalist' about time. This position about time will be argued for, *via* criticisms of the alternatives, in the second-to-last chapter.) Suppose for instance that the total mass of the universe, though huge, is finite. Then consider the possibility of some mass that is greater than that finite mass. Is not this mass, though not instantiated, a property? No, I say, it is no more than a *possible* property. And a possible entity is not automatically a reality. You can see that this follows from the rejection of 'abstract objects', objects that are additional to space-time. In the case given the merely possible mass is not instantiated in space-time. The natural conclusion for a one-worlder such as myself (one of those who reject the reality of other possible worlds), is that it is a *mere* possibility, one without instantiation.

But can one uphold universals and still reject 'abstract entities'? Are not universals, even instantiated universals, abstract from their very nature? To answer this query we must distinguish between two sorts of universal: 'Platonic' and 'Aristotelian' we may call them. (I won't worry about the scholarship here.) The Platonic view makes its universals 'abstract' or heavenly objects, but an Aristotelian account, which I favour, 'brings them down to space-time'. (There is a slight complication here, which will be picked up when we come to the discussion of states of affairs. See Chapter 4.) It is natural, I think, for an Aristotelian theory to reject uninstantiated universals.

A Platonist view, by the way, might find it necessary to have both universals *and* the corresponding tropes. The universals – the Forms for Plato – would be abstract, while spatiotemporal objects would have trope properties: sphericity might exist abstracted from space-time because for Plato nothing in the ordinary world is perfectly spherical. But individual billiard balls would each have their own trope near-sphericity, that is, they will have sphericity to a certain degree of approximation.

A further conclusion that I draw from my discussion is that properties are *contingent*, not necessary beings. Perhaps there are some properties that are necessary – in logic and mathematics, say – but I am dubious even there. The old line of thinking, introduced by Plato I think, is that universals are very splendid objects, and so are naturally thought of as necessary beings. My idea is to deflate their dignity and see them on the same level as particulars, which are generally thought of as contingent beings.

A bit more explanation is required here. The distinction that philosophers make between necessary and contingent

is naturally drawn in the first place between necessary and contingent *propositions*.[2] It is therefore a logical distinction. A true proposition, *p*, is contingent if and only if its contradictory proposition, not-*p*, though false, is not *contradictory*. In this minimal sense, not-*p* is *possible*. A necessary proposition, *q*, is one where its contradictory, not-*q*, *is* self-contradictory. But it would seem that with respect to *what is proposed* by the two true propositions – the somethings in the world that exist to make the propositions true – there will have to be an ontological difference. Thus arises the idea that we can distinguish between contingent beings or states of affairs, on the one hand, and necessary beings or states of affairs, on the other. This view is accepted by many metaphysicians, and I myself regard it as fundamental to my sketch (though some, such as Quine, reject the whole distinction between contingent and necessary as misconceived). But those of us that do accept the distinction maintain that ordinary objects or states of affairs are contingent beings and that empirical science issues in contingent truths about them, including the laws of nature. Necessary beings or states of affairs, however, are studied in the so-called 'rational sciences' of logic and mathematics. There are problems here that we will have to pick up at a later point of this essay, but here we will restrict ourselves to the idea that universals are *contingent* beings. It is *possible* that they do not exist, in the minimal sense that this possibility does not involve any contradiction. It may be idiotic to deny that you, the reader, exist, but since you are a contingent being, there is no *contradiction* in the denial.

---

[2] A theory of propositions will be put forward in Chapter 7. I connect propositions with *intentionality*, and thus with the mind. I do not think that there is an ontological realm of propositions as some philosophers hold.

Notice that it is sometimes said by logicians that that the notions of necessity and contingency are inter-definable, so that both are not required. But their definitions have to use negation and from the point of view of metaphysics the word 'not' brings up very difficult ontological problems that we will be confronting later in this book.

The important point here is that all universals must be instantiated by particulars somewhere and somewhen. Once one has this in mind it can be seen that there seems to be no contradiction in supposing that a certain candidate for being a universal (say Plato's perfect circularity) is nowhere instantiated, although it might have been. With no 'abstract objects' the best we can say is that that there is a possibility of instantiation in space-time but no actuality. This makes universals contingent beings.

We come now to a point that is perhaps the most important modification that needs to be made to get a satisfactory theory of universals. Traditional theories of universals allowed, or tended to allow, universals corresponding to most general words and general concepts. (There is an analogy here with Predicate Nominalism.) The idea was that one can pretty much read off universals from descriptive predicates. I reject this, and this rejection, I'm happy to say, has been widely accepted (among those who accept universals). When David Lewis came to accept property classes, or tropes, or universals (while not choosing between the three positions) he used the word 'sparse' to indicate that he accepted the getting away from an uncritical use of predicates to pick out these classes, tropes, or universals. 'Sparse' is a very useful word here. It tells us that in postulating universals we should not postulate them promiscuously.

The central idea of a universal is that it is a one (the one property in the monadic case) that runs through many particulars. (Though there is a limiting case – a universal that is instantiated by just one particular. I'll argue later in Chapter 4 that there *must* be at least one such case.) In his *Philosophical Investigations* (1953, Sec. 66) Wittgenstein appears to be criticizing the notion of particulars having something in common with his example of *games*. He has been understood as criticizing the notion of a universal. No doubt he is right about games. There is no universal of 'gamehood'. It is far too sprawling and messy a concept. But that will not disconcert the upholder of a sparse theory of universals in any way.

But how do we determine what the true universals are? My suggestion is that they are best postulated on the basis of *total science*. If so, universals and scientific realism need have no quarrel. (I think that this point was also accepted by David Lewis.) This makes the giving of examples speculative and difficult, especially because the true universals may not be identified until, say, we have a completed physics! But I think that the class of the masses: kilos, ounces, tons, and especially the more sophisticated units in which mass is measured may form a class of universals. They can do as examples, at least.

At the same time, though, even when doing philosophy, we often need to refer to properties that are not universals, for instance *being a game* or *being a householder*. I call these 'second-rate' properties. I hope that they are not an ontological embarrassment. My idea (my hypothesis) for dealing with these properties is to deploy a supervenience thesis. Suppose you had a God-like complete account of the world organized as the instantiations of all the universals, both properties and relations. Then, I suggest, you would at the same time

have, with no ontological addition to the world, all the instantiations of the second-rate properties and relations. I don't know how to prove this, but it seems to me to be plausible. It is a case of 'nothing over and above' – always an interesting claim because it gives us the more ontologically economical theory, a virtue if one can get it.

My metaphysics is based on particulars that instantiate universals. But it should be noted that the distinction between particulars and universals has been challenged by some thinkers, famously by Frank Ramsey (Ramsey [1925] 1997) and recently by Fraser MacBride (MacBride 2005), who cites Ramsey. Ramsey's logico-linguistic arguments are complex, but I believe that the most that they show is that one might reasonably deny the distinction. I don't think that they show that a metaphysics that uses the distinction is thereby invalidated. I think that within the system I am putting forward there is a clear enough distinction, as I will now argue.

For me particulars are confined to space-time and universals are all instantiated by these particulars. Given this, following a suggestion by Daniel Shargel, we can say that particulars are things that are subject to change, actual or possible, but universals are not. This becomes evident when we notice that we have a ready understanding of counterfactuals involving change to a part or a property of a particular. It is easy to imagine that one might have been a little shorter than one actually is, or somewhat less irascible. But counterfactuals involving change of universals are very artificial, especially if the universals involve laws, as will be argued at a later point. In this way we can come to see that Plato was right to connect universals with the permanent and particulars with the changeable, even if (as I think) it was wrong to place the Forms outside space-time as he did.

We may end this chapter on properties by calling attention to a useful distinction introduced by W.E. Johnson, that between *determinable* and *determinate* properties (Johnson 1921). Johnson works out the formal distinction very carefully, but only a sketch seems necessary here. Examples of determinables are the properties having colour and having mass. Colours such as red, blue, green, and yellow are determinates relative to colour, but red, for example, is a determinable relative to scarlet, crimson, and so on. Absolute determinates are reached with absolutely precise shades of colour. The absolute determinates of mass are, for instance, the ounce, pound, kilo, each taken precisely. It is a mark of determinates falling under the same determinable that a particular having one of these determinates cannot have any of the other determinates. If some surface is red all over then it is impossible for it to be green, if it weighs an ounce it cannot weigh a pound. This distinction between determinables and determinates will be important when we come to discuss laws of nature.

Determinates are clearly rather good candidates for universals. If you take a scientifically respectable property such as mass, then it is the mass determinates that it is natural to take as universals. Strict identity is essential for universals, and it is plausible, at least, to think that each particular that has mass of one kilogram exact is identical in that respect. But it is much less clear that determinables are universals. They are very useful properties because they collect determinates, say the mass determinates, into a rather unified class. But they do not seem to point to something that is strictly the same in each member.

There are further reasons for thinking that universals must be sought among determinates. If you consider some actual physical situation with bodies interacting, say on a billiard

table, in considering what the causal outcome will be one needs to think only of the determinates of these bodies, their determinate mass, motion, relative situation, and so forth. The determinables seem to play no extra role. Consider also that a determinate – mass 10 kilos say – entails, necessitates, the determinable for that property. Do we want a body to instantiate *two* universals, the determinate mass and the determinable of *having mass*? The second property seems an unnecessary extra, it supervenes on the determinate mass, and so is no addition of being.

In my first treatment of universals I accepted this outlawing of determinables as universals (1978b, Chapter 22, Sec. 1). But in my 1997a, considerations from the nature of laws of nature led me to reinstate determinables as universals. I now think my first idea was correct. I leave this aside for the present, however, until the chapter on laws of nature. It is quite a teasing matter. In the meanwhile we have the distinction between determinables and determinates, which I think Johnson was right to make.

More still can be said about the very rich and important theory of properties. It is a central metaphysical topic. But this more is best postponed until we discuss states of affairs.

Chapter 3

Relations

Coming to the topic of relations, much that has been said about properties can be repeated. Indeed, the word 'properties' is sometimes used by philosophers to cover both properties and relations. Here also a sparse set of relations may be identified as universals. For a relation to be an existent it must be instantiated at time and places. The distinction between determinables and determinates applies: say the distinction between distance and one metre exact distance. It is the determinate relations rather than determinables that are the natural candidates for universals. What the universals are we must wait for total science to tell us, just as in the case of properties.

These resemblances between properties and relations are no accident. I think we should adopt Russell's idea that properties and relations form a series, with properties the first or monadic case, then dyadic, triadic relations, and so on (we can call them the polyadic cases). But here we come to something more controversial. After we get past the monadic case, I think a quite important principle kicks in (at least for the relations that are universals). I call it the *Principle of Instantial Invariance*. For each universal U, if it has n terms in one instantiation, then it has the same number (n) in all its instantiations. My idea is that the number of terms a universal has is part of what that universal *is*. And a universal requires

strict identity in its different instantiations. So, I think, it should have the exactly the same number of terms in each instantiation.

This has been disputed by Fraser MacBride (MacBride 2005), an article to which Jacob Berger called my attention. The Principle of Instantial Invariance treats the adicity (a word for the number of terms in the relation) as an essential property of a relation that is a universal. But MacBride suggests that, if there are universals at all, the adicity could be a non-essential property of a universal, varying across instantiations. MacBride is right to raise this possible objection: I should have argued the point. But I still think that Instantial Invariance is the more plausible. To deny it is to admit some rather strange extra states of affairs, and perhaps strange possibilities, into the ontology. Particularly strange, it seems to me, is that a universal be in one instantiation a property in the strict sense, and at the same time be, say, a five-term relation in another instantiation. But I have been arguing that it is an *a posteriori* matter to decide which properties are genuine universals and it may be that completed science would rule against me here. (By the way, the word 'term' here has nothing to do with language. It just refers to the number of particulars that the relation relates. It is an unfortunate ambiguity in philosophers' usage.) There are, of course, relations that do not obey the demand for Instantial Invariance. A case suggested by Noa Latham is *being the tallest among*. For me, this would show that this relation is not a universal, but is instead a second-rate relation.

There is a really important distinction to be made now between what I call internal and external relations. (NB. There are other senses for this vocabulary of 'internal' vs. 'external' relations.) An internal relation, as I define it, holds

solely in virtue of the nature of the terms. Given the terms, the relation is necessitated. Thus: '12 is greater than 7' is an internal relation holding between numbers, 'Sydney is 500 miles north of Melbourne' is an external relation. It is the external relations that are the important ones ontologically. The traditional cases of external relations are the great majority of the spatiotemporal relations and causality, although necessitarian theories of causation may affect this classification. In the case of the internal relations it would appear that the relations supervene on the related terms, that is, when you are given the terms of the relation, you are given the relation. I'd construe this as showing that such relations are not an ontological addition. (They are an ontological free lunch!) The objects that stand to each other in internal relations could be in completely separate spaces, yet still internal relations could hold between them – relations of resemblance and relations of difference in particular. Resemblance is a notorious instance of an internal relation. There is, for instance, no objection to relations of resemblance between objects in different possible worlds.

This chapter has been short. I do have the feeling that there is a good deal more of importance to be said about the metaphysics of relations, but am unable to make any further contribution.

Chapter 4

States of Affairs

It is time to introduce *states of affairs* or *facts*. (In my usage 'states of affairs' are always existences – though not for all authors.) The instantiation of a property universal is the simplest type of instantiation. With *a* as a particular and F a monadic universal we have the state of affairs *a is F*. With R as a two-term relation we have the state of affairs *a R b*. (Philosophers use the upper case to stand for properties and relations, lower case for particulars.) Russell treated monadic facts as the single-case fact and as no more than the first case of a series which continues as dyadic, triadic, etc. I follow all this. Universals that are relations must, of course, be instantiated as much as properties.

This enables us to understand the Aristotelian 'putting universals within space-time'. You don't take space-time and *then* pour in your universals! Rather, you accept the thesis that the space-time world is a huge and organized net of states of affairs, some monadic, some of higher adicity, so getting universals into the structure of the world. (Notice that states of affairs are also available for trope theorists, if they want them.) I think that these states of affairs are, like their constituents, *contingent* existences. There is no contradiction in denying their existence.

There is a big puzzle in the notion of instantiation. It sticks particulars and universals together. Some have spoken

of a *fundamental tie*. That sounds like a relation, but it seems to go deeper than a relation. After all, if you took, say, a dyadic external relation that related two particulars, then the terms of the relation and the relation seems to demand a tie, just as much as the monadic case. But if the tie is itself a relation, you will need a further tie to tie the second tie in, and a regress of ties of the sort that F.H. Bradley pointed out in his classic *Appearance and Reality* ([1893] 1946) will be up and running. This threatened regress, by the way, is probably the best argument that a Nominalist about properties has.

What must first be done, I think, to deal with this problem is to take states of affairs as *the* fundamental structures in reality. They are primary, particulars and universals secondary. I mean by this that states of affairs are the least thing that can have *independent* existence. Unpropertied particulars and uninstantiated universals are false abstractions, meaning that they are incapable of independent existence. But the situation remains puzzling. I will make a new suggestion at the end of this chapter for resolving the problem.

Something interesting to notice is that states of affairs – *a's being F* and so on – are particulars. The combination of particulars and universals in a state of affairs yields a particular. I call this 'the victory of particularity'. The phenomenon had already been spotted by Russell (Russell 1949). He writes:

There are thus at least two sorts of objects of which we are aware, namely, particulars and universals. Among particulars I include all existents, and all complexes of which one or more constituents are existents, such as this-before-that, this-above-that, the-yellowness-of-this.[1]   (p.213)

---

[1] This quotation was brought to my attention by Albert Kivinen.

From this, as I will argue shortly, we can conclude that the world is a particular, not a universal.

We come now to a first brush with negation, a permanent trouble for metaphysicians! Suppose that *a's being F* is a state of affairs. Should we admit a state of affairs *a's not being G*? I reject negative states of affairs. But suppose it to be true that *a* is not G, then I concede, indeed assert, that this truth requires a truthmaker. That will be matter for a later chapter, where I will appeal to *totality* states of affairs (Russell's 'general facts') to do the job. If we reject negative states of affairs, though, then we must also reject negative universals. If F is a universal, then *not being F* is not a universal, although the *predicate* 'not being F' is a perfectly good predicate. Notice also that there might be a positive universal X that happened to have the very same extension as the class of non-Fs.

How do we decide what are the positive properties? Not by semantics alone. I think it is an empirical matter, which of course is close to the idea that universals have to be identified *a posteriori* on the basis of our best science. The notion of a vacuum is an interesting one here. A vacuum is, verbally, space with nothing in it. But physics tells us that all sorts of things are present in a vacuum, particles, and perhaps magnetic or gravitational fields if you are a realist about fields. So perhaps vacuums are not as negative as seems implied by the word. There also some tricky cases where philosophy may have to make the decision. Consider the terms 'identical' and 'different'. 'Different' means 'not identical'. But is difference the negative notion? Peter Simons is one philosopher who thinks difference is the positive notion (personal communication). It does seem to me to be the less empty term, though I have no clear argument.

What about disjunctive states of affairs (say, *either a is F or a is G*) and with these, disjunctive properties (*either F or G*)? Neither of these do we seem to need. (Though science might surprise us here.) If F and G are both universals is *being F or being G* a universal? I don't think so. But I am inclined to accept *conjunctive* universals. If *a* instantiates universals F and G then F&G is a universal, I think, though there is disagreement about this. I have two arguments for this view, though they are not conclusive. (i) The conjunction passes a very important test for a universal: it is a one that is strictly the same in its different instances. (ii) There seems to be the epistemic possibility, that is to say, 'a possibility for all we know', of conjunctions 'all the way down'. F and G, perhaps, are themselves conjunctions of universals and so on without end. This situation would make it necessary to accept conjunctions of universals as being universals, but how we could ever have good evidence of such infinite structures is admittedly hard to see.

An important sort of universal, of which a conjunctive universal would be a simple case, is what I call a *structural* universal. It can be illustrated by reference to the methane molecule, M, which, let us assume for our purposes here, is a universal, *being a methane molecule*.

$$
\begin{array}{c}
\text{H} \\
| \\
\text{H}-\text{C}-\text{H} \\
| \\
\text{H}
\end{array}
$$

Here we have a single carbon atom connected by different instantiations of the *bonding* relation B to four hydrogen atoms. Suppose B, C, and H are each of them universals. Then M is a structural universal, involving universal properties and relations, B, C, and H, which we may call *constituents* of M.

(There is the epistemic possibility of structures all the way down.) It is very important to notice that structural properties themselves enfold states of affairs. The four bondings in the diagram above between hydrogen atoms and the one carbon atom are each states of affairs of a certain sort.

As a matter of fact though, H, C, and M are somewhat dubious cases of universals. Molecules and atoms are *kinds* of things, and the metaphysical status of kinds is not entirely clear to me. Kinds usually involve very complex structures – think of kinds of animals, of plants, even of kinds of cells, and all the different sorts of parts that they have – and it becomes uncertain whether all the members of a particular kind have something *identical* running through all of them, the mark of a universal. Perhaps there are particulars that can meet this strict condition – quarks, say, or other fundamental particles – but macroscopic kinds seem dubious. There is something property-like about kinds, but strict identity (or the parallel notion of exact resemblance in a trope philosophy) may be beyond them.

I favour, a bit uncertainly, a supervenience thesis about kinds. Suppose we are given all the particulars with all their (universal) properties and (universal) relations. Then, perhaps, the kinds supervene, that is, are nothing over and above the properties and relations of things.

We can pause here to note the biggest structural property of all, of which there can only be one instantiation. Consider the whole of space-time (multiple big bangs and all, if there are many big bangs as some cosmologists now think likely) that I hypothesize to be the whole of reality. Take all the particulars, past, present, and future, with all their non-relational properties and all their relations to each other. (It may well be that there is an infinite number of states of affairs,

though the infinity – up or down – is not an established fact.) This constitutes the biggest structural property. We can't begin to spell it out but it seems it must be there. It involves, as constituents, every lesser state of affairs. The lesser states of affairs therefore supervene on it because they are enfolded in the all-embracing property. (Of course, it might have been bigger or smaller – it might have been different in all sorts of ways.) This property has just one instance. I like to call it W. There is a particular, call it w, that instantiates this property. The state of affairs that embraces the world is *w's being W*. And that is also a particular, by the 'victory of particularity'. The world is a particular as well as being a state of affairs.

Going back to the distinction between the relational and the non-relational or intrinsic properties of particulars, it is, as already argued, the latter, the intrinsic properties, that are the really important properties of particulars from the point of view of metaphysics. In our ordinary discourse we do not mark the distinction at all clearly. Think of predicates like 'mother', 'father', 'sister', and 'brother'. They, it is clear, involve relations, causal relations as it happens. Such descriptions are socially very important for us. But they are not intrinsic properties. And from the standpoint of metaphysics it is the intrinsic properties, shape, size, mass, chemical constitution, and so on, that are central. The relational properties of particulars are in some sense superfluous. Suppose that we are given all particulars and their intrinsic properties and that further we are given all the external relations (the relations that do not involve in any degree the intrinsic properties of the related things). Then we do not need the relational properties of objects as any sort of extra. The relational properties supervene.

Here is another way to make the point. The intrinsic properties of things are, in a somewhat stretched but real sense, *parts* of the things. Ordinary parts are *bits* of things, the totality of the bits making up the thing. Intrinsic properties are not like that, but they do make a contribution to the make-up of the thing. They are parts in a stretched sense. Relational properties, however, are not *anything* like parts. I think it is clear, then, that there is a big ontological difference between intrinsic (non-relational) properties of objects and their relational properties. This is a bit obscured by the fact that the distinction is not very clearly marked in ordinary language.

Let us now go back to the really central notion of the fundamental tie, the tie that brings together particulars and universals to give us states of affairs. I have a new suggestion to make. Hume argued, in effect, that it is impossible that there could be necessary connections between (wholly) distinct entities. The principle is quite attractive, and many empiricists have upheld it (including myself). But I am now going to suggest that we could relax it a little. Suppose we allowed there to be necessary connections *in re*, in the world. In particular suppose we were to postulate an objective necessity holding between particulars and universals. We might well make the connection to be of a limited sort. It might be no more than this. Universals (contingent beings as I think) need not have just the instantiations that they actually have. But they must (an anti-Humean *must*) be instantiated by particulars, at least once. Particulars (contingent beings) need not have the properties they actually have. But they must (an anti-Humean *must*) instantiate universals. There would then be a mild necessary connection between particulars and universals, and this would be the 'fundamental tie' that

so many metaphysicians have felt it necessary to postulate. Particulars and universals would retain their distinctness while needing connection with the other. States of affairs would remain contingent beings.

I don't know how to back up this suggestion except as an *inference to the best explanation*. It explains the mysterious nature of the fundamental tie that holds the constituents of states of affairs together, thus giving us the states of affairs, and it rids us of uninstantiated universals and particulars, objects that have no intrinsic properties, no intrinsic nature, no natural place. They do this with a minimal (though real) departure from the Humean distinct existence principle.

I'll finish this chapter by considering two points. One difficulty was raised by Wade Martin, also a graduate student at CUNY. How, he asked, do we differentiate one property from another? Would I not be forced, he asked, to postulate properties of these properties in order to do the job? But it is clear that this would lead to a most unpleasant regress of properties.

I think that answering this query leads to an important consideration in the theory of properties. If we use the word 'property' to include relations, then the different adicities would mark off many properties from each other. Consider then two properties that have the same adicity. How do we differentiate them? Some perhaps are complex and so have a structure. Difference of their structure will differentiate them. But there may well be *simple* properties with the same adicity, say all monadic. How do we differentiate them? In my book *A World of States of Affairs* (1997, 10.41) I put forward an idea that I still like: such properties would be *numerically* different only. Many philosophers have argued, rightly I think, that it is possible, though perhaps it never actually occurs, that

two particulars, two spheres say, could have exactly the same properties.[2] My suggestion is to extend this to properties. Suppose, for instance, that the two properties are monadic and simple. Then I propose that although they are different, they are numerically different *only*.

The second point is this. Wittgenstein said at 1.1 in his *Tractatus* that the world is the totality of facts, not of things. I think he was here echoing (in a striking way) Russell's idea that the world is a world of facts. I put the same point by saying that the world is a world of states of affairs. To say that the world is a world of things seems to leave out an obvious point: how these things hang together, which must be part of reality. Interestingly, my own teacher in Sydney, John Anderson, used to argue that reality was 'propositional' and appeared to mean much the same thing as Russell and Wittgenstein. One could say metaphorically that reality was best grasped as sentence-like rather than list-like.

[2] See the classical paper by Max Black, 'The Identity of Indiscernibles', 1952.

Chapter 5

Laws of Nature

Once you have universals in your ontology, one starts thinking rather naturally that one might use them to cast light on
the topic of laws of nature. After all, the laws are the fundamental ways in which things behave, and ways of behaving
depend on the properties of things. And if properties are
universals, laws should somehow connect the universals that
particulars instantiate. In the seventies of the last century the
very same idea came to three persons: Fred Dretske, Michael
Tooley, and myself. After all, why not give an account of
the laws of nature as *direct relations between universals*? We all
published within a year of each other, Dretske and Tooley in
articles, myself at the end of the second volume of my 1978
book on universals. That was a remarkable manifestation of
the *zeitgeist*: the spirit of the times that impels different people
to come up with the same idea quite independently. We had
no connection with, or influence on, each other. Dretske's
article in *Philosophy of Science* (1977) was very straightforward
and is an ideal article for a student to read first.[1] Tooley's fine
but more difficult paper appeared in the *Canadian Journal of
Philosophy* (1977). I went on to produce a book *What is a Law
of Nature?* which came out in 1983.

---

[1] I once said to Dretske that his paper was so useful because it presented the
theory before it became 'sicklied o'er with the pale cast of thought' (Hamlet).
This was taking a risk, but Fred was not offended by the joke.

The driving force for all three of us was dissatisfaction with the then reigning 'Humean' account of laws which, if we put it in the context of a 'states of affairs' metaphysics, holds that laws are merely regularities in the connection of these states of affairs. They supervene on the totality of these states of affairs. Lewis refers to the view as the thesis of Humean supervenience. He gives the classical treatment – building on the work of John Stuart Mill, and then Frank Ramsey ([1925] 1997) – the Mill-Ramsey-Lewis account of laws. Laws are a systematic and organized set of regularities in nature, nothing more. (For detailed critique of this position see the first part of my book *What is a Law of Nature?* (1983). I argue that it has many weaknesses.)

Let's take one often quoted case that lets us see the rather implausible *lack of strength* in the Humean supervenience view. Consider and contrast a mass of uranium 235 and a mass of solid gold. Make the masses rather large – say the size of some ordinary house. We know that there are no such masses. But in the uranium case we think that this is a nomic (law-like) affair. The mass of the uranium would be way above critical mass and so would have to explode and destroy itself (or at least this would be overwhelmingly probable). What about the mass of gold? We know that such a mass does not exist and almost certainly will never exist. But there does not seem to be anything in the laws of nature that would rule out such a mass of gold. There is something a bit accidental here. There may not be any way to collect so much gold, and in any case there is no reason to deplete the rest of the world's gold in this way. But it seems to be *nomically possible*, that is, it is not ruled out by the laws of nature. The M-R-L theory struggles with this point.

But what the three of us suggested for laws was a *non-supervenient direct link* between universals. Suppose that all Fs are Gs, with F and G universals, then this will suggest (but certainly not entail) that there is a direct link between the two universals such that *being an F* ensures *being a G*. (This is a toy example – in reality the situation will be far more complex than this, but it should help to grasp the move we made.) I symbolized the relation as a higher-order universal, the relation of 'N'. So we have the nomic state of affairs N(F,G), additional, not supervenient on, the first-order states of affairs. 'N' was chosen as standing for nomically necessitates, but this necessitation was taken by all of us to be a *contingent* relation between the universals involved. The idea is that N(F,G) should entail that all Fs are Gs, although there is no entailment in the reverse direction.

You can see how this enables one to say something very interesting: that laws *explain* what happens. Fs are observed, and they are all observed to be Gs. We explain the observation by postulating that there is a direct connection between the property F and the property G. This is a case of what is often now called *inference to the best explanation*.[2] We go from the regularity to the laws that explain the regularity, though not deductively. Humeans can't do that. You don't *explain* a mere observed regularity, which is all they allow, by postulating that the regularity holds for unobserved Fs, in particular by future Fs.

It is to be noted further that this gives some handle (I'm not sure how much) on the famous *problem of induction*, the problem of getting from observation to the unobserved.

---

[2] The phrase 'inference to the best explanation' was first introduced by Gill Harman (1965). A whole book on the topic has been written by Peter Lipton, 2nd edition, 2004.

By giving an explanation for the observed regularity, the 'connection of universals' theory gives some reason to believe that the regularity will hold for the unobserved instances of F. Hume and Humeans, however, have no basis for the belief that the future (or more generally the unobserved) will resemble the observed.[3]

Nice work if you can get it. But a great many philosophers have asked what is the warrant for the inference, which must be an entailment, from N(F,G) to the state of affairs that all Fs are Gs. Is it not established by simply assuming it must hold?[4] One sign that seems to show that something has gone wrong is to ask what happens if we have a law of nature that involves like ensuring like. Newton's first law of motion would be a case in point. A body in uniform motion and not acted upon by a force ensures that the same motion is maintained. Wouldn't we need to symbolize it as N(F,F)? But a universal linked to itself sounds crazy. In my 1997a book, I finally found a way to explain the situation. But I cannot blame Stephen Mumford for saying in his book (Mumford 2007, Chapter 3) that my new explanation is a new theory. I'm glad to say he thinks it is a better theory.

It is states of affairs that should be appealed to in the first place. We need the notion of a *state of affairs type*. If *a* is F then the corresponding state of affairs type is *something's being F*, which we can symbolize as:

$$\underline{\qquad}F$$

---

[3] See my paper 'What makes Induction Rational?', 1991a, for further discussion.

[4] By far the most penetrating criticism came from Bas C. van Fraassen in his paper 'Armstrong on Laws and Probabilities', *Australasian Journal of Philosophy* 65 (1987), 243-60. I replied in the same journal in 1988: 66, 224-9, but I did not then have available the notion of states of affairs *types*.

If we consider a dyadic state of affairs of a's having R to b then it can be symbolized as

$$\_\_ \ R \ \_\_$$

It is easily seen that states of affairs types supervene on states of affairs, and so come at no ontological extra cost. Perhaps, indeed, one can identify these states of affairs types with universals (it makes the need that universals have for particulars very clear) but I don't think we need to settle the matter here. Perhaps it is just a verbal matter, anyway. It then seems natural to bring in *causality*. The link between the states of affairs types seems to be a causal one. But I will leave commenting on this point just for the moment.

Suppose, now, that a's being F *causes* b's being G. (Absurdly simplified. F and G are universals, of course.) The corresponding state of affairs *type* can be symbolized in the following way:

$$\_\_1 \text{ being F causes } \_\_2 \text{ being G.}$$

The numbers are there to indicate that the connection runs between two different particulars. It is plausible that the first particular, a, must stand in some particular relation – say, a spatiotemporal relation – to b. That's what you would expect in ordinary cases of causation. You would have

$$\_\_1 \text{ stands in (spatial) R to } \_\_2$$

with the same two particulars picked out by the numbers. Given that spatial R holds between 1 and 2, then something of the *type* 1 causes a state of affairs of *type* 2. Here will be a crude model of a causal connection holding between universals. And because the connection is between types it will ensure that the connection is law-like.

It will then be seen that this dissolves the problem posed by that puzzling N(F,F). If we analyse this in terms of states of affairs types, there is then no objection to:

$$\underline{\quad}_1 \text{ being F causes } \underline{\quad}_2 \text{ being F.}$$

1 and 2, for instance, might be successive time-slices of a continuing thing or process, something that we will look at shortly.

But notice that a jump has been made. It is an ontological hypothesis that there are states of causal connections of the sort just indicated that link states of affairs types. What I plead for the hypothesis is that it gives us a plausible way of saying what laws of nature are, while denying that they are just regularities. If you don't think that there are laws of nature (perhaps because you believe in *powers* instead) then you don't have to accept this analysis. You must, of course, have universals in your ontology to work this trick. But is it not a *reason* for having universals? You can't turn the same trick with tropes.

One may be troubled by the suspicion that not all laws of nature are causal laws. It is a bit troubling, I would concede. Perhaps the conservation laws that play such an important role in physical theory are not causal laws. Causal laws *ensure* (or make probable to a particular degree) a certain outcome. But perhaps there are ensurings that are not causal.

But now for some delightful rewards. We have in the previous chapter touched on *structural* properties. So now I suggest that the laws of nature as symbolized above are themselves a species of structural universal. They are universals that involve causal connections, but that does not seem to be an objection to their being universals. There are plenty of structural connections – supportings, holding things in

place, for instance – that seem to involve causality of some sort – why should not some structural universals involve such causal connections? In the case of the methane molecule previously discussed the *bindings* of the four hydrogen atoms to the carbon molecule are certainly causal.

If laws are a species of universal, then, according to me at least, they have to be instantiated at some place and time. Well, we talk of laws being instantiated, do we not? (The points where the laws are 'operative'.) So this instantiation of laws is the instantiation of a special sort of universal. (Note that this would require every law to be somewhere instantiated in space-time.)

Now for a further point. The instantiations of the law, I now assert, are *all there is* to the law. The law, being a universal, is *completely* instantiated at every point where it is instantiated. It is instantiated in the singular case. And there is nothing else to the law. One consequence of this is that there cannot be laws that are never instantiated. But one might have a case like this. Suppose that one has certain instantiated laws, and that it can be *deduced* from these laws that if certain boundary conditions occur, that is, if there are certain distributions of particulars of a certain sort, then certain results will follow. But suppose that these particular boundary conditions never obtain in the whole history and geography of the world. Then, perhaps, one would have a secondary sort of law for conditions that never occur. One might call them counterfactual laws.

So, I claim, with the help of universals and the device of states of affairs *types* we have been able to define what we might think of as an intermediate necessity, intermediate between Humean contingency and necessity. We might call this 'nomic necessity'. We can easily adapt this account to

deal with the situation where laws are merely probabilistic. One might simply subscript the nomic necessity with a figure between 0 and 1. If the laws involved are causal laws, then one can interpret this as *probability of causing*. I say 'probability of causing', rather than 'probabilistic causality'. My idea is that the word 'cause' can remain univocal here. Causing, where it occurs, remains the same. A probability of causing is, I suggest, a probability of *ordinary* causing. It is just that the causing does not always happen, although conditions for it are ripe. Such a probability of causing would, of course, have to be an objective feature of reality, which some might object to.

A shortcoming of what has been said so far is that the laws, or hypotheses for laws, that science actually works with are functional affairs, regularly expressed in equations. If you consider, for instance, the Newtonian law of gravitation (for simplicity), you see that it covers a huge number of empirically possible cases: different masses at different distances with a general formula (for two objects at different distances: $F = M_1 \times M_2/D^2$. This leads to a difficulty that I did not originally notice.

If you consider the gravitation formula immediately above it will be evident that F, M_1, M_2, and D are determinables not determinates, to use the terminology explained at the end of Chapter 2. The symbols are variables that range over the different forces, masses, and distances that may be involved in actual states of affairs. In my *World of States of Affairs* (1997a) I suggested that this should be explained by going back on the idea that determinables could not be universals. Functional laws should be accepted as connections between *determinable* universals.

The trouble about this move, though, is that there seem to be a number of reasons, explained in Chapter 2, for thinking

that these properties are not universals. It is, for instance, determinate properties that are actually operating in causal interactions between particulars. My present view, therefore, is that the determinables are not universals, as I originally argued. So what becomes of the idea that laws of nature are connections between universals (states of affairs types)?

We have to say, I think, that functional laws are bundles of what we might call *particularized laws*, laws that hold for determinate properties, determinate forces, masses, and distances in the case of the gravitation law. The determinables, very important properties but not universals, when suitably connected by some mathematical relationship, give, as it were, 'instructions' for the particularized laws where the work of the world is done.

This account does lead to a consideration of 'missing values' in the case of particularized laws. May there not be determinate values for functional laws that are never instantiated in the whole history of the universe? We can think up possible cases. Suppose that the world has a finite mass. Then we might still think that if it had a greater mass than it actually has, still one might think that a gravitational law might apply to such cases using the formula supplied by the law. The result would be a *counterfactual*: if masses of such a sort were instantiated, then a certain upshot would have occurred. For scientifically good reasons, one might be inclined to assert such a counterfactual. Would this case need uninstantiated universals as truthmakers for these truths, assuming them to be truths? Platonists might like to think this way. I'd prefer a more economical solution. The truthmaker would be the connection between the determinables properties that explains the observed connections in the actual cases. Given the law plus the imaginary case, the outcome is

determined. That is the reason for calling the counterfactual a truth.

Causation. We have introduced a new theme in this discussion: causation. The Humean account of causation (leaving aside the question whether this was Hume's own view, a matter that is disputed by historians of philosophy) is that *token* causality, say this particular impact that pushes over this glass of water, is causality only in virtue of the fact that what has happened is the same all over the universe. What makes the token sequence causal is a *relational* property of the sequence for Humeans. The opposite view is that token causality is an *intrinsic,* non-relational, property of the token sequence. The metaphysical choice here can be seen as like a *Euthyphro* question, like the question whether the goodness of an act is determined by some relational property (such as a certain sort of approval) or by the intrinsic nature of the act.

It is very plausible, I think, that the causal relation is intrinsic, intrinsic to its token pairs, and this is my view. This makes me a *Singularist* about causation. Such a view is compatible with the idea that instantiations of laws of nature are instantiations of connections holding between states of affairs types. The simplest hypothesis, and the one I accept, is that singular causation *is* nothing more than the instantiation of some law.[5] This is a theoretical identification. It remains rather a moot point, as already mentioned earlier, whether every instantiation of law is a case of causation, a point about which I am uncertain. My inclination is to think that if this is not so, the point does not mark some major ontological

---

[5] For details see my article 'Going through the Open Door Again: Counterfactuals versus Singularist Theories of Causation', Armstrong 2004b.

distinction between laws that do, and laws that do not, involve causation. But this may be wrong.

The acceptance of the singular causation raises a very interesting epistemological question. Can we perhaps *perceive* causation, perceiving it in the direct sort of way that we perceive colours, shapes, distances, and other sensible qualities and relations? We could hardly do this if a Humean account of causation is correct because it would be magical to be perceptually sensitive to vast regularities over space and time. The best one could do then is to make some sort of inference from bodily sensations. But if causation is singular, then there seems to be an obvious candidate for perception: the action of various forces upon our body. This is information that we need for the immediate conduct of life and if it is lacking we would be most grievously handicapped. Relevant here seems the case described by Oliver Sachs of the woman in 'The Disembodied Lady' (in Sachs 1986) who suffered total loss of her proprioceptive capacity (perception of her own body), leaving her with almost no information about the state of her body save what could be painfully and artificially gained by vision. She could not be directly aware of the action of the world on her body. But we luckier ones are so aware, and so, it seems plausible, are aware of causal action on our body. Of course, even if my suggestion here is correct, we would not be experiencing the operation of a causal law. What we experience when we experience the operation of causes on our body will be the mere *resultant* of the causes operating upon some portion of our body at that time.

You can put the point by saying that among our sense impressions should be included sense impressions of some of the forces that act upon our body. David Hume, it may be

remembered, argued that all our ideas (concepts) are derived, directly or indirectly, from sense impressions. But he says that he is unable to find any impression of causality, and in particular he denies that there is any impression of the *necessary connection* between cause and effect. All the senses give us, he assumes, are regular successions. I think that this is very likely quite wrong. In Humean terms, there are impressions from which we can derive the idea of causation. There are such impressions, impressions of forces acting on our body. Impressions can err, of course (error is always possible in perception), but in veridical cases we are able, I claim, to perceive causal action on our own body. (And we don't have to think, as Hume seems to assume, that this would have to be a necessary connection. It could be contingent.)

Incidentally, Hume also denies that we experience causality in connection with willing our actions (in many places in his *Treatise* and *Enquiries*). I think he may be wrong here also. There seems to be direct introspective awareness of causes here, once again. We can be aware, with the usual caution that we might be mistaken, that we have successfully *acted* in a certain situation, that what we did sprang from our will as cause. (I'll try to cast some further light on this in the last chapter – about the mind.)

I have already suggested that the 'fundamental tie' might be construed as an objective necessity that universals must always be instantiated somewhere, and particulars must have properties. They need states of affairs to live in. It would be nice to have a further addition. Universals must be subject to laws, so must link up with universals in nomic (law-like) fashion in the way we have just discussed. But, at the same time, what particular laws the world obeys would be contingent. The attraction of introducing *this*

necessity into the world is that it would outlaw *epiphenomenal* universals – universals that exist, are instantiated, but have no nomic links to other universals, and so, according to my theory of laws of nature, no power in the world. How would we know of their existence?

Chapter 6

Reacting to Dispositionalism

So that was a sketch of my present version of the theory of laws of nature. But in recent years a line of criticism of this theory has been developed which demands consideration. The critique is associated with *power* theories of properties, a new, or rather a revived view, of what the nature of properties really is. It does not deny the existence of properties, indeed it insists on them, but it holds that they are powers, powers to cause certain effects. On that basis a critique is launched against David Lewis' neo-Humean view of laws of nature, and also on the 'connection of universals' theory. Important figures are Sydney Shoemaker in the US, Robert Black, Stephen Mumford and Alexander Bird in the UK, George Molnar (deceased, but see his posthumous book *Powers* 2003) and Brian Ellis in Australia, C.B. Martin in Canada (previously Australia), and a follower of his in this regard, John Heil, in the US. Some of these people uphold universals – the majority – and some uphold tropes, but that won't matter much to our discussion here. They are all regularly called 'Dispositionalists'. (The contrast is with Categoricalists – *not Categorialists* – the sorts of theory that the Dispositionalists try to displace.)

I must say something about dispositions in the first place. The word is a technical term in philosophy. Typical cases of dispositions that are used to illustrate the notion are solubility,

elasticity, and brittleness. Associated with dispositions are certain truths. Thus: if salt is put in water it will, in ordinary circumstances, dissolve. So salt is said to have the disposition *soluble in water*. If some salt is actually put in water and, as a result, it dissolves then this result is said to be a *manifestation* of the disposition. A very important point is that a particular quantity of salt may never manifest this disposition in the whole history of that quantity of salt. *Unmanifested* dispositions of particulars are perfectly possible, and, indeed, it is normal for particulars to have dispositions that are never manifested in the whole of their history. There is now a large philosophical literature on the topic of dispositions. It is a plausible thesis that in every case of cause and effect the effect can be seen as the manifestation of some disposition or dispositions, and such a view would be a congenial one for a Dispositionalist.

But the Dispositionalists go a great deal further than this. They wish to resurrect the old pre-Humean idea of *powers*. Powers may be *necessitating* or *probabilistic*. A necessitating power is a deterministic one, and where the power manifests itself there is a *necessary connection* between the power and its manifestation. The Humean idea that there is no necessary connection between wholly distinct existences is completely rejected, much more than my cautious qualifying of that idea at the end of Chapter 4. If the power is such that it gives only a *probability* of manifestation in suitable circumstances, something that seems to occur at quantum level, there remains of necessity an objective *chance* of a manifestation of the power in question. Perhaps all powers are a bit chancy in this way, but that is a matter for physics. Notice, by the way, that Dispositionalists can take their powers to be universals or to be tropes, and being philosophers they naturally divide on the issue of tropes vs. universals!

One problem that the Dispositionalists face is to give an account of the laws of nature, for them the laws (or perhaps they would prefer to speak of equations) that govern the operation of powers. That is not a question that they have yet turned much of their attention to. But it gives an occasion to go back to the account of laws of nature that I favour. What account of dispositions should the universals theory give? On particular occasions dispositions are manifested. These manifestations will be explained without difficulty because they will be explained by appeal to the laws of nature. All the universals theory has to do is to give an account of *unmanifested* dispositions. My suggestion is that such dispositions are no ontological addition to the world. An object, say a drinking glass, begins to fall towards a stone floor, but it is grabbed before it reaches the floor. The brittleness of the glass is fortunately not manifested on this occasion. But can we not identify the unmanifested disposition with the nature of the glass, that is, with one or more *properties* of the glass? The Dispositionalist may respond that these properties are themselves dispositions. But that would be to beg the question against the Categoricalist position I am defending. The property of the glass in virtue of which it is brittle is likely enough to be a structural property, involving the fundamental particles that make up the glass and the laws of nature that govern the spatial interrelations of the particles, but the view I am defending is that these are ultimately categorical. It is likely, also, that various counterfactual propositions are true in the situation, for instance, 'if you hadn't grabbed it so quickly, then it would have broken'. But these counterfactuals, I think, though true, are not true in virtue of any ontological addition to the world. This last point will be discussed later when we come to consider the ontology of possibility.

But let us return to the discussion of Dispositionalism. Causes have certain properties and it is in virtue of these properties that they produce effects ('manifestations' for a Dispositionalist) also having certain properties. But what will these properties be? Must not the Dispositionalist say that they are dispositions? The following picture emerges. There are particulars having certain dispositions that act in virtue of these dispositions, that is, are causes. They produce certain effects, manifestations, and they are dispositions also. We seem to be in a world consisting of particulars that have dispositions *and there is nothing else there.* It is a world of dispositions, or rather, because Dispositionalists in general do not try to reduce particulars, it is a world of particulars having nothing but dispositions. This, I think, is a sort of nightmare. One might call on external relations between particulars to add something that is not dispositional in nature. But the thoroughgoing Dispositionalist, instantiated by Sydney Shoemaker (Shoemaker 1984), will dissolve relations into dispositions also. Dispositionalists talk of manifestations, but a manifestation that is nothing but a disposition to produce manifestations that are dispositions to produce manifestations that are . . . seems to me to be a very unsatisfactory metaphysics. It may not involve a contradiction, but that seems not enough of a merit.

Relations, moreover, look to be a particular stumbling block to this position. Can they be brought within the scheme? In the Newtonian case it is fairly easy to think of the masses involved as mere powers. But how do we handle relations such as distance? If they too are powers, what will their *manifestations* be? Two things moving towards each other? But two things moving towards each other hardly seems to be a power, which it ought to be if Dispositionalism is a correct view.

There is, however, a line of criticism, inaugurated by Robert Black, which has been launched against Categoricalists (Black 2000). Black accuses us of *Quidditism*, of being landed with properties that do no real work in the world, and so constitute a serious weakness in our metaphysical position. He focuses on the contingency of the laws, which the universals theory holds to in common with the Humean position. Here is how his argument goes. Suppose that the law connects universals F and G in a certain way and another law links H and J. He points out that in another possible world things might have been different. Universal F, say, might have been linked nomically to J, and H linked to G. This we Categoricalists must accept because it follows from the contingency of the postulated connections. But, the argument continues, this need not involve any difference in the way the world would work. Everything else would go on all the same. This, Black argues, shows up a striking lack of economy in the universals theory. Dispositions, however, are essentially causes, so they do not, he argues, have to be hooked up *via* these mysterious categorical properties.

While jibbing at 'mysterious' I think that the universals theory has to accept the case. Such a scenario is a possibility. But it is a *mere* possibility, comparable to the possibility that the world began five minutes ago, or will come to an end in five minutes' time, or for that matter the possibility that the world is really Humean, though appearing to be governed by strong laws, a 'possibility' that the universals theory has always cheerfully accepted.

It may be noted, also, that some Dispositionalists, in particular Ellis (2001) and Molnar (2003), appreciate the implausibility of a complete Dispositionalism. They exempt

spatial properties and relations in particular. Their positions are thus a mixture of Dispositionalism and Categoricalism (Quidditism). So they are in no position to push Black's argument. (Ellis, incidentally, makes *kinds* central in his Dispositional scheme.)

Chapter 7

Particulars

During our discussions so far, caught up as we have been with universals and the difficult topic of laws, we have not paid much attention to particulars: sticks, stones, trees, animal and human bodies! So we should now consider their nature. They persist through time, and we consider them one thing during that time. But I don't think we should take this too seriously. This is because I don't think that this involves *strict* identity through time. (To use contemporary jargon, the view advocated here is a *perdurantist* rather than *endurantist* account of the identity of particulars over time.)

I think that we can with advantage here go to a distinction drawn by the 18th century bishop and philosopher Joseph Butler between what he calls the *strict* sense of identity and a 'loose and popular' usage of words where something much less strict is demanded. He uses it in his discussion of the identity of objects such as trees over time. He writes:

For when a man swears to the same tree, as having stood fifty years in the same place, he means only the same as to all the purposes of property and uses of common life, and not that the tree has been all that time the same in the strict philosophical sense of the word. For he does not know, whether any one particle of the present tree be the same with any one particle of the tree which stood in the same place fifty years ago. And if they have not one common particle

of matter, they cannot be the same tree in the proper philosophic sense of the word *same* . . . .   ([1736] 1906, pp.258–9)

Butler applies this idea in his discussion of the identity of particulars over time (pp.258–9). It is very plausible for innumerable cases. Any macroscopic particular will be changing the whole time, yet we will be happy to say in most cases that it is still 'the same particular'. There are of course cases where the change is so great that we will not be prepared to speak of sameness of particular even in this 'loose and popular' sense. If a drinking glass shatters into a myriad of small pieces, there is no drinking glass left. Ideally, conditions for 'loose and popular' identity would need to be spelt out. But that is a rather detailed investigation that will not be pursued further here. Notice that this sort of loose identity will very often apply to the gaining and losing of parts of the particular in question. But also note that there may be *fundamental* particles that make up ordinary particulars where these particles stay the same in a more fundamental sense of sameness, exactly the same, just as Butler allows.

So I think that the identity of an ordinary particular is only this 'loose and popular' identity that Bishop Butler refers to. After all, if the states of affairs theory is correct, as I have argued, then at any particular time (each *time-slice* of the object in the jargon) the particular is a hugely complicated state of affairs, and furthermore is in perpetual flux. If you really want the unchanging particular instead of a temporal 'bit' of the object you need, I suggest, to consider the object four-dimensionally, as a 'space-time worm' to use yet another bit of jargon.

But that is only a beginning. After all, all sorts of space-time worms exist in space-time and only a few of these will be

what I have called particulars. You can 'draw lines' arbitrarily in space-time in the fashion of a space-time worm and yet not capture anything that we would think of as a particular. What marks off ordinary particulars? First, continuity of existence plays an important part (though there are objects that are disassembled periodically and then reassembled). There is, in general, spatial continuity over time. Second, resemblance is important, especially between nearby slices, and where there is change in nature that change should generally be not too abrupt. But although these things are important there is something more hidden, that seems of great theoretical interest: it is causality. There ought to be causal links that link together the successive temporal segments of the continuing thing. Russell in his unjustly neglected book *Human Knowledge: Its Scope and Limits* (1948) went so far as to call particulars *causal lines*. I think he was right.

What is the argument for this causal binding together of successive parts of a particular? The compelling argument comes from considering the negative case. Suppose a space-time worm that has continuity of the right sort and where the continuous slices closely resemble each other. But suppose that there are one or more *causal breaks* at certain times in the existence of the supposed particular. At these points there is absolutely no causal (or other nomic) connection between what goes before and what comes after. I think we would not be prepared to say that it is 'the very same thing' before and after. Instead what succeeds is no better than a mere simulacrum of what went before. (One can imagine annihilations and replacements, ones not causally connected in any way, occurring at the break points.) Particulars are always changing in some degree, but while the particular exists it must *grow causally* out of its past.

Can we say more about the nature of the causation involved? I think we can. W.E Johnson, who we have already noticed for the distinction between determinable and determinate properties in his three-volume *Logic,* also drew a distinction between two types of cause (Vol. 3). He called the one *transeunt* causation (going across), and the other *immanent* (remaining within). Transeunt causation is the more ordinary sort of causation, when one thing brings about something in another particular (or *sustains* something, as when supporting something or keeping it in existence) and it can be argued that it is the only sort of causation that there is. But I think that immanent causation is also actual. Spontaneous emission from an atom of uranium 235, radioactive decay, might be such a case. It is spontaneous because not produced by causal action from outside the atom. It doesn't matter that probability rules in this emission case. Probabilistic causation is causation when the law 'fires'. Does the 'spontaneous' suggest that there is no causation here? Well, it obeys a probabilistic law so why should it not count as a case of the uranium atom causing one of its constituent electrons, say, to be emitted? It is this sort of causation that I take to be operating when a thing persists. Russell does not speak of immanent and transeunt causation, but does link immanent causation with Newton's first law (Russell 1948, p.475): 'a body at rest remains at rest unless acted upon by some force'. (And equally can we not link transeunt causation with Newton's third law: 'action and reaction are equal and opposite'?) Immanent causation, if we accept it, will generally be a monotonous series of happenings where like produces like.

Recapitulation. So far I have sketched the main themes of my metaphysics. The world can be identified with

space-time, with 'space-time' operating as a placeholder for the cosmic reality that cosmology and fundamental physics seek to discover. It is best understood, I have argued, as a world of states of affairs (Russell's 'facts'). Although states of affairs involve particulars and universals, these 'constituents', as they may be called, are not capable of existence independently of states of affairs. Particulars and universals necessarily involve each other, an ontological necessity that lies at the heart of states of affairs, and so lies at the heart of reality. It is to be noted that these states of affairs are particulars, a point already appreciated by Russell (the 'victory of particularity' as I call it). Particulars are contingent beings – there is no contradiction in denying their existence – and since universals must be instantiated, universals and states of affairs are contingent beings also.

Universals are either *monadic* or *polyadic*, that is, they are properties or relations. Note that philosophers sometimes use the term 'property' to cover relations also. We can resolve this ambiguity, when it needs to be resolved, by speaking of monadic universals as 'non-relational' or 'intrinsic' universals. There is room for *complex* or *structural* monadic universals, whose constituents may involve relations, and even for the epistemic possibility that every universal is complex (structures all the way down). I have argued for the somewhat controversial position that relations that are universals are *instantially invariant*, that is, that they link the same number of terms (particulars) in every instantiation. Relations may be divided into *internal* and *external*. (There may, of course, be mixed cases.) The ontologically important relations, such as distance in space or time, are the external ones, that is, relations that are *not* necessitated by the terms involved. Internal relations are relations that hold of necessity

in virtue of the nature of the terms, the related things. They constitute no ontological addition to their terms.

Laws of nature hold in virtue of the universals involved in the states of affairs between which causal or other law-like connections appear to hold. In particular, they may be seen as connections that hold between states of affairs *types*: say, *something being F* bringing about that something, or, more realistically, some further being that stands in some spatial relation to the original something, bringing about *something's being G*. Such an account seems to generalize reasonably smoothly to the all-important quantitative laws and equations of empirical science. It also lends itself to a *Singularist* account of causation, but one where the instantiation of a law is an instantiation of the universals involved in the nomic (law-like) connection. Laws exist in their instantiations and nowhere else, and so are universals themselves, even if a rather special sort of universal. The account allows for a new justification of the inductive step from observation to the unobserved. It is an *inference to the best explanation* from the empirically observed instances to the 'strong law' that explains the regularity. It is, though, a *further* type of state of affairs in addition to the states of affairs that were originally postulated. (It is a *general* state of affairs in Russell's terminology.) But be warned: there is still another type of state of affairs to come before this sketch ends.

Universals are not to be postulated *a priori* nor on mere semantic grounds. There is no one–one correlation holding between general terms in our language and universals. Universals are to be postulated on the basis of our best empirical science.

But there is much more to be done if we are to have something that constitutes a systematic metaphysical position.

Many questions have to be answered. What about modality?: what is the nature of necessity, actuality, and possibility? What about the distinction between the realm of the *a priori* (mathematics and logic) and the realm of the *a posteriori* (empirical science)? What ontological problems are posed by the existence of these two bodies of knowledge? The latter, the *a posteriori*, perhaps does not lead into any major problems for my empiricist metaphysics, though the conflict insisted upon by Wilfrid Sellars, the *manifest* image of the world, the world of perception and common sense, on the one hand, and the *scientific image* presented to us by physics and cosmology, is real and pressing. (Something will be said about this in the last chapter, on the mind.) But here we can perhaps pass this by to be dealt with not in this sketch but by a comprehensive epistemology, though an ontologically directed epistemology. Before dealing with this, there are problems raised by the universal quantifier, and what is not quite the same thing the word 'all', the concept of totality. And there are still greater problems raised by negation and the word 'not', problems that have constituted a sort of fascinating nightmare for metaphysicians. These problems are now the subject of further discussion.

Chapter 8

Truthmakers

In my view the most promising development in recent metaphysical discussion has been the emergence of *truthmaker theory*. The truthmaker of a particular truth may be initially defined as that particular entity in reality in virtue of which that truth is true, and the force of this definition will emerge, as I hope, in the rest of this book.

A short historical account will not be inappropriate. The perhaps rather odd-sounding term 'truthmaker' (which I write without a hyphen) was coined twice, once by C.B. Martin (Charlie Martin) in the years when he was in Australia, where quite a lot of attention was given to the topic; and a second time by three English philosophers, Mulligan, Simons, and Smith in an article they published in 1984.[1] Martin's work was particularly interesting because he concentrated on counterfactuals (truths such as 'if he had read the warning, there would have been no accident' where he did not read the warning) that various philosophers used without making it clear what the truthmakers for these counterfactuals were.[2] Though there appeared to be no common cause, it was clear that the term was being used in exactly the same sense by the Australians and the three Englishmen. The two bodies of

---

[1] 'Truth-makers', Mulligan, Kevin, Simons, Peter, and Smith, Barry, 1984.
[2] See my *Truth and Truthmakers*, Chapter 1, 2004a. Chapter 2 discusses general principles that I argued should govern truthmaker theory.

thought flowed together harmoniously, at least to the extent that philosophers can be harmonious in their thinking.

We should notice, though, that Russell can claim to be the originator of truthmaking theory. In *Human Knowledge* (p.166) he speaks of the

... fact or facts which, if they exist, make a belief true. Such fact or facts I call the 'verifier' of the belief.

He never develops the point very far, and in any case 'verifier' is most unfortunate terminology. To a generation of philosophers in flight from the dreadful Verification Principle advocated by the logical positivists (roughly, a truth must be verified, or at least be verifiable, to be a truth) 'verifier' smacks of a theory that they are trying to get away from.

In my view truthmaker theory should be seen as a development of the correspondence theory of truth, the utterly naturally idea that truths are true if and only if they correspond to something in reality. Truths are made true by the real. The special contribution of truthmaker theory is the point that the correspondence of truths to reality need not be a one–one correspondence to reality. Consider for instance the truth that at least one human being exists. We don't need just one thing to be what makes this truth true. The relation is a one–many relation. Each human being that exists is, just by itself, a truthmaker for this truth. That is an easy one. But finding truthmakers for certain sorts of truths can be a difficult and controversial matter, as will emerge. Consider, for instance the truth that there is no elephant in the room. What is the truthmaker for this?

There are many good philosophers who make good use of truthmaker theory but deny that every truth has a truthmaker. They might deal with the elephant in this way. They are

not, as I am, a *truthmaker Maximalist*. But I think that this Maximalism flows from the idea of correspondence and I am not willing to give up on the idea that correspondence with reality is necessary for any truth. (By the way, do not confuse truthmakers with truth conditions, which will not be discussed further here. Truth conditions are just propositions thought to be important truths about selected entities, whereas truthmakers are realities, existences.)

One important thing to appreciate about the truthmaking relation is that it is an *internal* relation. The nature of the truth and the nature of whatever it is that makes the truth true are the only things involved in this relation. It is rather easy to overlook internal relations – there are so many of them and they are usually not of great interest. This may help to explain why the truthmaking relation is rather easily overlooked. In my view, then, having a truthmaker is not an optional extra but of the essence of what makes a truth true.

Those philosophers who work with truthmakers, but reject truthmaker Maximalism, face a certain problem. What theory of truth do they accept for the truths that lack truthmakers? As far as I know they have not discussed this problem. It seems likely that they would accept for these truths some version of a minimalist theory. The theory goes back to Frank Ramsey's paper 'Facts and Propositions' (F.P. Ramsey 1927). Ramsey observed that to assert that 'it is true that Caesar was murdered' is to assert no more than 'Caesar was murdered'. We can say 'what she said was true' and this saves us having to repeat her words. 'True' seems little more than a term of convenience on this view. A contemporary version of the theory is argued for by Paul Horwich in his book *Truth* (1990). The view of truth is minimalist. That so little can be said about such an important notion as truth is a reason to suspect this theory.

Returning to truthmaker theory, a quite important notion is that of a *minimal* truthmaker. (Nothing to do with the minimalist theory of truth!) A minimal truthmaker is one that is a truthmaker for a certain truth *with nothing to spare.* Sometimes where it is difficult or controversial to hit on a minimal truthmaker, it is useful to produce a less than minimal truthmaker. And it may be noted that every truth has *the whole of the world* as truthmaker, though indeed it is an uninteresting truthmaker, at least for most truths. It is also worth noting that if there is infinity anywhere in the world (a question to which I think we do not, perhaps even cannot, know the answer) then there are truths that *cannot* have a minimal truthmaker. Suppose that there are an infinite number of electrons in space-time. The totality of the electrons would be a truthmaker for this truth. But every second electron would also be a truthmaker or every nth electron provided n is a finite number, with no minimal truthmaker. (This elegant point was spotted by Greg Restall, 1995.)

The truthmaker for the truth 'at least one human being exists' is easy to decide. But the assigning of truthmakers can be a very controversial matter, even among truthmaker theorists. This is because the postulating of truthmakers is a move in metaphysics, and so is inevitably controversial. But such postulatings will be found of great use in our inquiries, even if they do no more than make more clear just what point is being contested. To ask a philosopher what his truthmakers are in some field should remind us of Quine's suggested question 'What do you quantify over?' To ask for truthmakers may be a better question than Quine's.

That will do as an introduction to truthmakers. But we need to consider also the other side of the truthmaking

relation: the *truthbearers*. I hold the perhaps orthodox view that the truthbearers are (true) propositions. But what are propositions? My view here may be less orthodox. I do not, as some philosophers do, believe that there is a realm of propositions that has 'abstract existence' in addition to space-time. I think that propositions are best understood as what appears after such phrases as 'believes that', 'supposes that', 'entertains the thought that', 'doubts that'. There is something abstract about propositions, but abstract in a more ordinary way than Quine's 'abstract objects'. I identify propositions as what is believed, what is supposed, entertained, doubted, etc. It is important to notice that propositions in this sense can include *impossibilities*. Hobbes believed that he had 'squared the circle'. But his purported construction of a perfect square with exactly the same area as a given perfect circle was a believing of something that is impossible. (Philosophers have a technical term for propositions of my sort: they call them 'intentional objects' of belief, supposition, etc. We shall meet them again in a discussion of the mind in the last chapter.)

Notice again that the truthmaking relation is an internal relation in the sense already introduced: given the terms, the truthmakers and the propositional truthbearers, the relation is given. The truthmakers, I think, necessitate the truths, that is, the truthbearers. This seems to be a matter of supervenience. Reality fixes the truths as true.

The Entailment Principle. I call attention here to a very important principle that flows from truthmaker theory. Suppose that a true proposition *p entails* a proposition *q*. By truthmaker Maximalism *p* has a truthmaker. According to the Entailment Principle, it follows that this truthmaker for *p* is also a truthmaker for *q*. It may not be a *minimal* truthmaker even if

the truthmaker for p is minimal. Note that this *must* be an entailment. If all that is true is that $p \supset q$, the so-called material conditional, then this result does not follow. Note also the importance of truthmaker *Maximalism*. If Maximalism is false – say it is false for negative truths as many philosophers hold – then the application of the Entailment Principle must be correspondingly limited. But entailment is transitive – it carries on – if p entails q and q entails r then p entails r and so on. This will prove to be important for our discussion of numbers and classes.

Something rather interesting can also be drawn as a consequence of the Entailment Principle. Philosophers have suggested, and it is quite an interesting idea, that in a valid argument (one that follows by necessity) the premises already contain the conclusion (though we may fail to make the deduction). This can be recast in truthmaker terms, where the matter seems clearer. In a valid argument the truthmaker for the conclusion is contained in the truthmaker for the premises. The conclusion needs no extra truthmakers. We will have much use for the Entailment Principle in the remainder of this essay.

One thing I wonder about is the status of this agreeable Entailment Principle. It is clearly, if true as I think it is, a necessary truth. But what sort of necessity is this? Is it an analytic truth, or is it something deeper? As in the case of the link between particulars and universals in states of affairs, I now think it may well be a necessity that is ontological.

Chapter 9

Possibility, Actuality, Necessity

One way of coming to grips with David Lewis' theory of possible worlds (though perhaps Lewis would not have accepted the point) is that he is providing truthmakers for true propositions that something is possible. It would be an ontologically very expensive way of providing truthmakers for these truths. By contrast, I suggest that truthmakers for possibilities can be provided at very low ontological cost. Let us in the first place confine the possibilities to what I call *mere* possibilities. A proposition p is a 'mere possibility' if it has the structure 'p is possible but not-p is true'. (In standard symbols: $\Diamond p \& \neg p$.) Thus 'it is not the case that I am sitting' is false since I am in fact writing at my desk, but 'it is possible that I am not sitting' is a true modal proposition because it is *contingent* though true that I am sitting at my desk.

But we can use Maximalism and the previously discussed Entailment Principle to get a striking result. Consider the class, presumably an immensely large class, of the contingent truths. Each member of the class has associated with it a modal truth *of its own*, the possibility that it is false. That is true because that is what the contingency of the member *is*. It is true by definition. At this point the Entailment Principle can be wheeled in. The possibility that p is false plus the contingency of p entails 'it is possible that not-p'.

So the truthmaker T for *p* (Maximalism ensures that there is a truthmaker) plus the contingency of truthmaker T (the truthmaker of a contingent truth is a contingent being, as argued earlier) entail the truth of it is possible that not-*p*. So T together with its contingency are truthmakers for the 'mere possibility' that it is possible that not-*p*. That, I suggest, is all that is needed as truthmakers for the mere possibilities. Let us call this the Possibility Principle.

This simple but extraordinary result shows, I think, that current analytical philosophy, no doubt under the influence of the work of David Lewis, has greatly overvalued the ontological importance of the category of possibility. Another way, perhaps easier, to see the truth of the Possibility Principle is to consider that mere possibilities supervene on the actual. It is fairly easy to see that given the actual world, these mere possibilities, indeed all possibilities but especially the mere possibilities, come with it *automatically*, at no ontological cost.

Indeed, we are now saddled with a small new problem. What is the value of these modal truths? Could we not hold that there is nothing to the possible except what is actual? I think, though, that the notion of mere possibility needs to be retained, for pressing pragmatic reasons. Counterfactual conditionals, that is, 'if . . . then's with the 'if' clause false, play a very important part in the regulation of *conduct*. We have free will, at least in the minimal sense of being able, on occasions, to *choose* between courses of conduct. Choosing is a psychological reality. We can think that if we do X then in all probability Y will be the result, whereas if we do not do X in all probability Y will not occur. Doing X and not doing X cannot both occur perhaps (say, sitting down or standing up), so that one of them is a *mere* possibility. Afterwards, what was

actually done may give us useful lessons for what we should do if a similar situation should arise again. We are forewarned or forearmed as the case may be. So possibilities can be extremely important in considering lessons for future action. Again, the progress of science demands hypotheses, some of which inevitably turn out to be mere possibilities. Still further, the whole life of the mind, art, and culture involves continual trafficking in mere possibilities, as in storytelling and other cultural activities, some of which, paradoxically, can lead us to deeper truths.

It is worth noticing that counterfactuals are naturally entertained with respect to *first-order particulars*. This is because of the complex and easily varied and changeable nature of the particular space-time worms that we identify as particulars. It is therefore very easy to come to believe or entertain counterfactual propositions about such objects that turn out to conflict with later experience. Contrast this with universals, strictly identical in different instantiations as they must be, and subject to the laws of nature. It is not so easy or natural to entertain counterfactuals where the universals are thought of as different from the way they actually are.

So much for possibility as a metaphysical category. The actual can be dealt with fairly easily. The actual may be identified as existence, as being. There are, I think, no grades or levels of being. There is, as John Anderson at Sydney used to put the matter, just one way of being, a phrase I have heard on the lips of David Lewis after he had been introduced to this formula. And there are no non-existents. Notice that being, existence, has no special link to the present, and at a later point I will give reasons for rejecting the now rather widespread doctrine of Presentism, the position that only the present exists. The actual is of course possible, but this is a rather trivial entailment.

I turn now to necessity. What is necessary is actual, but, of course, what is actual need not be necessary, it can instead be contingent. Some necessary truths are analytically or conceptually necessary, though I do not think that this is the case for all necessary truths. I propose in the first place that the truthmakers for analytic truths are the meanings of the words or symbols in which these truths are expressed. We are all familiar with the point that analytic truths are not about meanings. The point is correct; that is not what they *refer to*. But being an object of reference is one thing, being a truthmaker is another. So my proposed truthmaker is in no conflict with the idea that analytic truths are true solely *in virtue of* the meanings of the words or symbols in which they are expressed. It is interesting to note that A.J. Ayer said *exactly* that about analytic truths[1] in his famous book *Language, Truth and Logic*. But because he had no inkling of truthmaker theory he was not able to see the depth of his own remark.

All of this, of course, is not to say how large or how small the class of analytic truths is. That class may be relatively small. That is something that remains to be settled, and it isn't all that easy to settle it. Nor does it give us any *theory* of meaning. That is a very difficult matter, as philosophers all know, and I have nothing to add here. But that words and symbols do have meanings is, I take it, a Moorean truth, a commonsense truth that we can hardly deny, though we can try to analyse it. Why then cannot we take these meanings to be the truthmakers for analytic truths?

Notice that these remarks seem to hold for conceptual truths also. They are true solely in virtue of the concepts

---

[1] 'I hold that a proposition is analytic if it is true solely in virtue of the meaning of its constituent symbols, ...' Ayer, 1947, p.16.

used to express such truths. Concepts here are taken to be psychological entities, but again I offer no particular theory of what they are beyond their mental nature.

But are all necessary truths analytic or conceptual? That is very hard to believe. I have already argued that the instantiation of universals and the rejection of unpropertied particulars constitute necessities that seem to be neither analytic nor conceptual, and with less confidence have suggested that any universal *must* stand in law-like relations to at least one further universal. I have also suggested that validity of argument may be something more than analytic or conceptual necessities. These necessities, if they are necessities, ought, I suggest, to be conceived as something ontological, a necessity in the nature of things. It seems possible that there are others. In particular there is the great, ever-growing, edifice of mathematics with its apparatus of axioms and proofs that yield a certainty that, if not absolutely certain, is the most certain knowledge that we possess. Can that all be merely analytic or conceptual? Surely some stronger truthmaker is required? Picking up here on a suggestion made to me in correspondence by Ross Cameron, may there not be foundational necessities that support these huge structures, even if these necessities are quite restricted in number? Non-contradiction, excluded middle, and perhaps other principles may be of this nature. It is for logicians to advise on the detail here.

The necessities which I suggest above are to be found in the world are all of them relational in nature. They link particulars to universals, universals to further universals, or proposition to proposition. But are there any *beings* that exist of necessity? There are candidates. Some philosophers hold, not only that there is a God but also that God is a necessary being. An interesting point here emphasized by Leibniz is

that if a necessary being is a possible being, then it exists. Just as a necessary truth is true 'in every possible world' so a necessary being would exist 'in every possible world'. Those philosophers who do not believe that there is a necessary being or beings, must therefore hold that a necessary being is impossible. That is the view that I support.

But there are other candidates for necessary beings, in particular numbers and other mathematical objects. Do not the natural numbers, say, and including the infinite cardinals, necessarily exist? I claim, however, that the only things that exist are *instantiated* numbers, numbers instantiated in structures in space-time: so many electrons, so many uranium atoms, so many human beings, and so on. Suppose that space-time is finite in every dimension, that there is no infinite collection of things and no infinite divisibility in things either. As far as we know this could be true. Then the infinite numbers would none of them be instantiated, and so would not exist. Planck's quantum (unit) of energy may point to the fact that nothing is infinitely divisible. It is no doubt *possible* that the infinities should be instantiated, but, as already argued, to be possible *and no more* is not to have being. The topic of number will be taken up again at a later point.

Could there be nothing at all? Philosophers worry about whether there could have been nothing at all. (One might reasonably wonder whether anybody but philosophers could take an interest in this topic!) Our reflections on the ontology of necessity together with the Possibility Principle can, I think, help us here. Note first that if there are any necessary beings, then a completely empty world is impossible. I've suggested above that there are no necessary beings, but even if this is mistaken there remains the question 'Could

there have been no contingent beings?'. Let us consider the presumably true proposition 'at least one contingent being exists'. It is very easy to find truthmakers. Any contingent being will do as a truthmaker! Then the associated modal proposition will be 'it is possible that not one contingent being exists'. By truthmaker Maximalism, this truth will have a truthmaker. By the Possibility Principle this truthmaker will be the same truthmaker as exists for the truth 'at least one contingent being exists'. So, if there are no necessary beings, then there could have been nothing at all, a truth that has a this-worldly truthmaker. The possibility is, as we know, a mere possibility. One can still, of course, ask *why* there is anything at all. In the event that the space-time world turned out to have an immanent teleology, a rather unlikely possibility I would judge but one I do not absolutely deny, we might even have a naturalist yet positive answer to this 'why' question.

I add a quick note on the modal but derivative notion of *impossibility* – the not possible. There are, of course, truths of impossibility, for instance 'it is impossible for something to be at the same time round and square'. It is gratifying to see how easily truthmakers can be provided for such a truth: the properties of roundness and squareness.

Chapter 10

Limits

We come now to one of the most difficult questions in metaphysics, a question that has been with us at least since the days of Parmenides. What should our metaphysics of negation be? Let us begin by looking at four attractive propositions put together in an article by George Molnar (Molnar 2000):

  (i)   The world is everything that exists
 (ii)   Everything that exists is positive
(iii)   Some negative claims about the world are true
 (iv)   Every true claim about the world is made true by something that exists.

These truths, it seems, cannot all be true together, which is why the putting of these four propositions together is so useful. Molnar offered no solution to the problem. (i) cannot be tinkered with, I think. (iii) seems plain commonsense – I am saying something true when I say that there is no rhinoceros present in my study. (iv) is truthmaker Maximalism. Although many philosophers who are sympathetic to truthmaker theory have sought to soften (iv), it is a proposition that I am most unwilling to give up. So I have to try to soften (ii).

Let us begin by introducing C.B. Martin's distinction between *limits* and *absences*. Limits set bounds to things – the persons in this room now, or to what exists, and all sorts of bounds, trivial or important, between these two cases. They

link up with the universal quantifier (∀) or more simply and accurately the word 'all'. Russell in the lectures on Logical Atomism called these 'general facts' but said he was not sure what the form of such facts should be. Absences are even more straightforward, the absence of a rhinoceros from this room, for instance. Russell called absences 'negative facts', and it was his arguing for these sorts of facts that he said caused a riot in the class when he put forward the case for negative facts in Harvard.

Russell later saw that one did not have to postulate negative facts — states of affairs — provided that one had a satisfactory account of general facts. General facts still involve negation — they could be called 'no more' states of affairs, so here is the point where I think negativity must be allowed. But our first task is to develop a theory of general facts, Martin's limits, which I shall call from this point on *totality states of affairs*.

Totality states of affairs. Because one can use the logician's quantifier '∀x' without necessarily implying that what is being quantified over, the x, exists, the quantifier is not quite right for our purposes. What we want really is just the ordinary word 'all' as in 'all the human beings in the world' or 'all the water on Earth'. To make true statements involving such phrases, there must be human beings or water. I call these 'totalities' or, using a made-up word, 'allnesses'. The first point to insist upon is that these totalities are perfectly objective. 'All the persons in this room now', for instance, is a perfectly objective totality as is 'all the water on Earth'. I've argued earlier that we are actually able to *perceive* causality, in particular in the perception of forces acting on our body or when we are aware of the operation of our own will. Now I point out that we can *perceive* totalities, in the strict

perceptual sense. For instance, we can look into a bird's nest and perceive that there are *just two* eggs at present in the nest. (A case suggested to me by Peter Anstey.) It may be in such a case that we are, unconsciously, using as a principle 'if there had been more than two eggs in the nest I would have perceived more than two eggs, but I don't perceive any more and am in a position to perceive the more if it were there, so . . .'. But ordinary perception is full of these sorts of 'animal inferences' as Russell called them (1948, pp.182 ff.). At any rate, as a result of my perception, I *know* that there are no more eggs in the nest, and this is Moorean knowledge, that is to say, it is very much more certain than any argument that a philosopher can bring forward to argue that we don't have knowledge in such a case!

So there are totalities in the world, objective totalities, and it seems that the ontologist ought to take notice of this fact. For the notion of a totality is a topic neutral affair and there are all sorts of totalities extending throughout being. It seems that there could even be infinite totalities, such as the totality of electrons. We don't know whether there are, or are not, an infinity of electrons, but either way there is a totality of electrons. There is even a totality, it would seem, of the natural numbers, an infinite totality that is less than the infinite totality of the real numbers, though this, as we will see later, demands care.

How do totalities and classes stand to each other? Some classes seem to be closely linked to totalities. By 'the class of electrons' we mean 'the class of *all* (and only) the electrons'. But 'all the water on Earth' is a totality that is not a class, though the singleton class of the object {all the water on Earth} is near at hand. (This was pointed out to me by Graham

Nerlich.) We will, however, leave aside a consideration of classes for the present.

If there are totalities, there are truths about them, and we can inquire what sort of truth they are. How should the truths be analysed, or at least what form do they have? And for somebody who is a truthmaker Maximalist, what are their truthmakers?

At this point it is convenient to introduce *mereology*. Mereological wholes and parts are the simplest sorts of relations of parts and whole. Their relations are given by the rather simple *mereological calculus*. For metaphysicians there is an ideal philosophical introduction: Chapter 1 of the book *Parts of Classes* by David Lewis (1991), though his monograph becomes difficult in the later chapters. A doctrine that Lewis puts forward, and that I accept, is quite useful for my argument here. It is the thesis of *unrestricted mereological fusion*. 'Fusion' is just the mereological putting together of two or more entities to make a whole. Fusion is unrestricted, any entities at all can be 'fused', that is, they can make a whole. The whole consisting of Sydney Opera House and the number 42 is a perfectly good fusion, as are any other entities. At the same time, Lewis argues, and I assent again, mereology is ontologically innocent. Take the fusion of some cats:

Mereology is ontologically innocent . . . The fusion is nothing over and above the cats that compose it. It just *is* them. They just *are* it. Take them together or take them separately, the cats are the same portion of Reality either way.   (Lewis, p.81)

Returning to totality truths, I re-emphasize that the pioneer in this whole line of inquiry was Russell in the *Lectures on Logical Atomism*. He called the truths involved *general truths* and said that corresponding to these truths general facts

are required, a special sort of fact (states of affairs in my terminology). However he said he did not know what the form of the fact was, though he would like to see the question studied. So here we are, ready to try to carry on his good work.

We can, it seems, pick out two aspects of these totality states of affairs. There is first the sort of thing that is being totalized, which we can call the totality's intension, and second there is the whole of the things collected, the extension as it is natural to call it. The first aspect would appear to be a property. But we can't make this to be a first-class property, a universal, except in very favourable circumstances. In the bird's egg case, there is a fact, a state of affairs, that these are all the eggs in the nest now. Of course there is no universal of *being an egg in this nest now*. But I think that will do for the property that does the totalizing. The extension, the whole, will be the mereological sum of the eggs in question.

You can think of the property as cutting the mereological sum up without remainder, like a cookie cutter. In this case, there is a neat division into two non-overlapping objects, the eggs. In some cases, though, there will be overlaps. In the case of all the water on Earth you won't get any neat dividing at all. But you do have a mereological sum of lots of bits of water that sum to the totality of earth's water, and there is a property handy: 'quantity of Earth water'.

Here is another way of thinking about it: the property totals ('alls') the mereological sum. This is a state of affairs, a relation that holds between the property and the mereological sum, but it is not a state of affairs of the sort we have met with so far. It seems needed, though, because the world is teeming with totalities. The world itself is a totality, the totality of existents or beings. Since we are not demanding universals, I

think we can accept *existence* (or perhaps positive existence) as a property for the world-total. (Neither existence nor positive existence are universals, it would seem. They are too general.) Alternatively we can go to the world-property, a property that we have already met. It picks out the world as its only instantiation, and this is a totality state of affairs.

A difficulty has been raised for these new sorts of states of affairs. Are they not *additions to being*? In the case of the world, to take it as an instance, does not the new state of affairs need to be included in what there is? There is the world, then, it is argued, there is a state of affairs that this is all there is. Don't you have to add it to the world? You can readily see that a nasty regress can then be produced that goes to infinity. It seems to be present for all totality states of affairs.

I used to have a solution, a bad one, to this problem. I accepted the regress but argued that the regress was a regress of propositions, but not a regress of beings. My model was the truth regress: if *p* is true, it is true that *p* is true, true that it is true that *p* is true, *ad infinitum*. But, I said, in the truth regress the *truthmaker* is always the original truthmaker for *p*. The truthmaker never changes as one keeps adding 'it is true'. I think all this is correct. But I then wrongly suggested that the same was the case for totality truths. (See my *Truth and Truthmakers* for this mistake: 6.3.1.)

I never quite trusted this solution. I now give a different answer. It seems to me now that I also had failed to see the point that totality states are *not* additions to being. *They introduce negation into the world.* They introduce it in the form of *limit*. They say of something *that's all*. If you claim truly that '*a* and *b* and *c* and *that's all*' you haven't added to the world with the 'that's all'. You have indicated that things are limited in some respect. The supposed first step in the regress

would be to bracket (*a*, *b*, and *c* and that's all), and then say again 'that is all'. But that seems to be nonsense. If you have (*a*, *b*, *c* and that's all) then adding another 'that's all' seems to get you nowhere, unless you are just referring again to *a*, *b*, and *c*. A fact of limitation does not add. It 'says' that after *a*, *b*, and *c* there are no more. That's not an addition of being.

An interesting case that may help to see my mistake is to consider the totality of being. It seems that there has to be an ultimate totality state of affairs, an 'everything' state of affairs. I accepted and still accept that there is such a state of affairs. But in the past it still seemed to me that this was an addition to the ordinary states of affairs, so I had to talk fast to try to prevent an infinite regress arising. But a cutting-off of all state of affairs is no addition. 'No more' is not something more! The cost is, a cost I suggest must just be paid, that negation in the shape of 'no more' must be admitted into our ontology. Limit is real. It is an ontological feature.

Philosophers don't like not-being. (Was Father Parmenides, as Plato called him, the culprit?) Russell said that his class at Harvard nearly rioted when he tried to argue for not-being in the form of negative facts. Maybe the class had a point if one is thinking about *absences* as Russell was then. But if you see them as *limitations* then I think you have to accept that there are such things. We even perceive them, as I have pointed out in the case of the eggs in the nest. So here is a new sort of state of affairs. It can be symbolized as Tot (property X, mereological whole of the Xs). That is its form.

One thing that may seem unsatisfactory about limit states of affairs is that at first glance they seem to falsify the Eleatic Principle, which seeks to find a (positive) causal role for everything that we postulate in our ontology. But if we avail ourselves of the rather wide interpretation of the principle that

the word 'role' gives us, maybe we can blunt this difference. Consider what would have happened if limits were not just where they actually are. Put one more, or one less, electron in the world. The new player or the absence of a player would change the game, a little at least, because it would have acted causally to bring about changes elsewhere (somewhere). Or that is what the laws of nature seem to tell us. So it, the actual electrons, all of them, make a difference, and so are responsible in some degree for the way the world goes. That, I suggest, is enough to say that *just that limit* has a causal role. These counterfactual truths would fail for epiphenomenal entities. But I've already suggested in Chapter 1 that if there are such entities we can know nothing about them, and so we may be entitled to assume that epiphenomenal entities do not exist.

Chapter 11

Absences

This brings us to the hard one: absences, which were what Russell was presumably arguing for at Harvard. To say that there is no rhinoceros in the room (indubitably true) goes beyond a limit and proclaims an absence. You might try saying that it really only limits the number of these animals, and so it is a limit fact. But you can't limit what does not exist, and a rhino in the room is a non-existent. If you worry that after all there are such animals and this room is simply off-limits to rhinoceroses, change the example to a unicorn. But I think the rhino case is an absence all right. 'There is only one rhino in the room', if that were true, would be a limit case, but 'there is no rhino in the room' is not.

Absences are really rather horrible, ontologically speaking. There are so many of them, and they seem never to have any causal power if you spell out the causal chains involved. Phil Dowe, in important work, distinguishes between *preventions* and *omissions*. With prevention a certain thing is prevented, and so does not exist. It is absent. With omissions something does not happen and so does not exist. It is absent. Dowe argues that both involve *counterfactuals*. The father grabs the child and so the child is not hit by the car. If the father had not done this, then the child would have been hit by the car. The non-existent thing that was prevented has no causal efficacy. Suppose the case is that the father failed to grab the

child, and so the child is hit by the car. The counterfactual is then reversed, the non-existent thing, the omitted thing, is grabbing the child. It also has no causal efficacy. We do use causal language in connection with preventions and omissions. But if we are concerned with ontology we should treat them as second-class cases of causality. (See, with much more useful detail, Dowe 2000, Chapter 6.) A further point is this. Suppose we are given all the real causal relations in the world. It seems that then we are automatically given all the preventions and omissions. They are nothing additional, they supervene. Consider, for instance, a billiard table with balls moving around it, sometimes hitting each other. Once you have all the motion of all the balls and their hitting each other then you also have the preventions and omissions that occur.

Limits, I've argued in the previous section, do seem to have some causal effects. They are better than absences in this respect. I think that we can use limits to curb absences. 'All' can be used to tame 'not'. But I'd be prepared just to accept absences into my metaphysics if the argument which I now present does not work. One thing I am going to use is the really instantiated but internal relation of *difference*. (Here I am to a degree following Plato in his discussion of not-being in his great dialogue *The Sophist*.)

Consider this room. There is no rhinoceros in it. How shall we provide a truthmaker for this truth? Given totality states of affairs we can do this. Take *all* of the room down to its most minute parts. The *all* is essential. Is it not true that *each* part of the room is *different* from a rhinoceros? The states of affairs that make up the room are all of them different from rhino states of affairs. Under these circumstances, there is no rhinoceros in the room. So cannot the room, *all* the

room, act as truthmaker for the truth that the room is rhino free? No bit of the room is a rhinoceros, however small the rhinoceros is.

There seems to be a problem if we change the example and say that there is no unicorn or centaur in the room. The trouble about unicorns and centaurs is that they don't exist and so, it would seem, cannot be terms for the relation of difference, which demands two terms. They can, however, be dealt with in a slightly different way, but one that still uses limits. Take the unicorns first. It is true that no horse-like animals are single-horned. So let us take as truthmaker the totality of horse-like animals. None of them is single-horned. They are each of them *different* from single-horned creatures. So this totality of the horse-like animals can be the truthmaker for the non-existence of unicorns, and *a fortiori* for their presence in this room. It is interesting to note that the totality of single-horned creatures (rhinos together with the other single-horned animals that there are) would also serve as truthmaker. We get two different truthmakers for the one truth. But I think that truthmaker theory need not worry about that. Truthmaking relations need not be one–one and in this case they are not. Two different truthmakers for the same truth, even two minimal truthmakers, is not objectionable.

The absence of centaurs from anywhere (and so from the room) can be dealt with in the same way. No humans are half-horses so the totality of humans can be a truthmaker for the lack of centaurs. The other truthmaker is the totality of the horses – none of them are half-human. One thing to notice is that, in general, very big truthmakers are required to be the truthmakers for negative truths. I think this helps to explain the difficulty of proving a negative. That you didn't

commit the crime, for instance, may require the totality of your acts on the fatal day as truthmakers. Hume remarks on the difficulty of proving a negative in his *Treatise of Human Nature*.[1] Now, we see, truthmaker theory is in a position to give an ontological explanation for Hume's epistemological insight.

One might think that for truths such as 'there are no unicorns' and 'there are no centaurs' the simplest thing to do is to offer the whole world as their truthmaker. Contemporary logic, after all, would offer us '(∀x) x is a non-unicorn' (or non-centaur) as the logical form of these truths, and these propositions are propositions about everything. And I would not deny that the whole world is a truthmaker for these truths. But is it a *minimal* truthmaker? I don't think so. Huge swathes of the whole world are really irrelevant to the non-existence of these animals. It is with the horses or the horned animals for the first truth, with the horses and the humans for the second truth, that the truthmaking action is found. I'm pointing to *minimal* truthmakers, of course.

Before leaving this section I'll come back to Russell. I might have known that Russell would be there before me. I think he made essentially the same point as mine, although he did not have the useful jargon of truthmakers, some time after his *Logical Atomism* lectures. It was in his introduction to the second edition of *Principia Mathematica* (p.xv). He saw the essential point that 'all' could be used to get round 'not':

Given all true atomic propositions, [*These are all supposed to be positive*] together with the fact that they are all, every other true

---

[1] Selby-Bigge edition, p. 212. Hume writes: 'I confess it will be somewhat difficult to prove this [a thesis of Hume's] to the full satisfaction of the reader; because it implies a negative, which in many cases will not admit of positive proof.'

proposition [*including the negative ones*] can theoretically be deduced by logical methods. That is to say, the apparatus of crude fact required in proofs can all be condensed into the true atomic propositions together with the fact that every true atomic proposition is one of the following: (here the list should follow). If used, this method would presumably involve an infinite enumeration, since it seems natural to suppose that the number of infinite propositions is infinite, though this should not be regarded as certain. In practice, generality is not obtained by the method of complete enumeration, because this method requires more knowledge than we possess.

I thank that redoubtable Russell scholar, Herbert Hochberg, for pointing out this passage to me.

Aliens. The truthmaker apparatus that we have now got enables us to deal with a teasing little problem, one that I mishandled over the years, the problem of what David Lewis called 'aliens'. It seems possible that there might have been properties and relations that do not exist in the world nor are combinatorially constructible from the properties and relations of the world. Again, there might have been particulars that do not exist in this world and are not combinatorially constructible from particulars that exist in the world. Lewis, of course, had a place for aliens, they were good citizens of other possible worlds. But what truthmakers can the one-world chauvinist such as myself give for truthmakers for what seem to be true modal propositions?

If we keep totalities in mind and the Possibility Principle, then the solution is not hard to discover. I will take a particular case. Suppose that there are simple properties, and consider the possibility, as it seems to be, that there might have been other simple properties besides the ones that exist. Collect all the actual simple properties (they might be infinite

in number, but still they have their 'fusion'). Remember
that properties are contingent beings. The proposition we
want to give a truthmaker for is the modal truth: 'there is
the possibility that it is not the case that this collection of
simple properties are all the simple properties.' Note that
this is not just an epistemic possibility. There actually are no
more simple properties, we are assuming. But the Possibility
Principle says that if p is contingent and has a truthmaker,
then that truthmaker is also a truthmaker for the modal truth
'possibly not p'. So the collection, the totality, taken as a
totality, is truthmaker for the contingent truth that these are
indeed all the simple properties. But then it will also be, by
the Possibility Principle, truthmaker for the possibility that
this collection is *not* the totality of the simple properties, i.e.
alien, extra, simple properties are possible (though not actual
by definition).

Chapter 12

The Rational Disciplines: Logic and Mathematics[1]

The disciplines of logic and mathematics are different from the empirical sciences. They issue in truths that are necessary and discovered *a priori*, and, with the exception of the axioms, they can be *proved*. All of this sets them apart from the empirical sciences, and creates problems for empiricist philosophers. A variant of Kant's question at the beginning of his *Critique of Pure Reason* then raises its head: how are these sciences possible? It is, though, a worry somewhat more extensive than Kant's question, which asked how is synthetic [non-analytic] *a priori* knowledge possible.

Quine denied that there is any such distinction among truths as the necessary/contingent distinction. But logic and mathematics seem to be sharply different from the empirical sciences. In these disciplines you can get *proof*, and get extensive *a priori* knowledge, but you can't do that in the empirical sciences (however much mathematics is used). We have to explain this difference. I suggest, against Quine, that we cannot explain it away.

---

[1] In recent years I have worked with Anne Newstead and James Franklin to defend an 'Aristotelian' philosophical account of mathematics. I'd call attention to their paper 'Indispensability without Platonism' (forthcoming). It strengthens the case for using truthmakers to denote metaphysical commitments rather than Quine's proposal to signal these by quantification.

I think it is right to think of pure mathematics as a science of *structures* but certainly not of any old structure. The structure must be completely abstract, that is, completely topic neutral. It may be quite simple, for instance a class, but it may, of course, be very complex. One particularly difficult sort of case, speaking philosophically, is the mathematics of the infinite. Cantor, using a beautiful diagonal argument, showed that the infinity of the natural numbers is a smaller infinity than the infinity of the real numbers. Apparently, we can know *a priori* that there is infinity in the world, and even that there are different infinities that can be ranked as greater or lesser. What is the empiricist philosopher to say about this?

My suggestion is that we ought to draw a distinction between instantiated and uninstantiated structures in mathematics just as I do for universals. The instantiated mathematical structures are instantiated at some place and time in the space-time world. It will be real things, concrete things, perhaps fundamental particles, that instantiate the mathematical structures. They are what exist. The uninstantiated structures do not exist. They are merely possible structures. The epistemology of the thing, determining whether a certain mathematical structure is or is not instantiated somewhere in nature could be horribly difficult. Leave that aside because it is not a problem we need to solve here (or elsewhere perhaps). But the ontological distinction seems straightforward.

We may call this position Possibilism in mathematics. It does involve a cost, the cost that an existence proof in mathematics gives us something less than one might hope for – it is only, I'm arguing, a proof of possibility. But it saves us from abstract entities! The hypothesis that space-time is the only existent can continue to be upheld (though of course not proved). I suggest that Possibilism should be extended even

to set theory. Does this Possibilism commit us to a potentially huge range of possibilities? Perhaps. But remember that we can appeal to the Possibility Principle argued for earlier to show that the ontological cost of *mere* possibilities, which are all that is needed, is not at all high. It is almost a free lunch.

But this by itself will not account for the *a priori* nature of proof. My suggestion for explaining this is to appeal to the Entailment Principle in truthmaker theory, which, it will be remembered, holds that if p entails q then a truthmaker for p is also a truthmaker for q (not necessarily a minimal truthmaker). Entailment is also *transitive*, we noted, that is if p entails q, and q entails r then p entails r. So if we have a chain of valid (necessary) deductions the truthmaker of the premise or premises will be truthmaker enough for the subsequent deductions, even if the chain stretches to infinity.

The getting of new results in these rational disciplines proceeds by *proof*, and the steps in the proof are necessary given the premises, i.e. we have entailment as the proof goes forward.[2] Then we can say that no new ontological entities are introduced by the proof. It is true that from time to time, perhaps in the course of the proof, new entities may be introduced, and defined. Perfect circles, for instance, were the subjects of investigation by the Greek mathematicians together with the number π. It may be that nothing in the space-time world, including the world, instantiates a perfect circle or instantiates π. If that is so, then strictly perfect circles cannot be part of our ontology. But they will still be possibilities. We can understand what the world would be like if they did exist, that is, if these expressions did have

---

[2] Even Gödel's famous incompleteness theorems for systems of axioms for arithmetic proceed by a deductive argument, that is, by *proofs*.

truthmakers. Then we can reason hypothetically, provided we reason deductively.

Some philosophers have suggested that in proof the proposition proved is contained in the premises. This is a suggestion difficult to evaluate. But if we shift to truthmakers we can shift to the claim that the truthmakers for true premises are sufficient truthmakers for the truths proved. This is a striking ontological economy, an economy given us by the Entailment Principle.

We do, of course, have to recognize that introducing the Entailment Principle drives us back to consider the axioms from which mathematical systems are developed. Given a set of axioms, we may argue that they are contingently true or contingently false, necessarily true or necessarily false. 'Necessarily true' is the particularly plausible view! There are then three possibilities, it seems. They might be analytically true, that is solely true in virtue of the meanings of the words or symbols used to state the truth. They might be conceptually true, true in virtue of the mental concepts used to express them. Or, finally, they might be true in virtue of principles that are fundamental necessities in the world, perhaps non-contradiction, excluded middle, and such like. The first two 'possibilities' are, I fear, too arbitrary and conventional. I have already found it necessary to postulate a necessity in the world to explain how particulars and universals demand each other, and so make states of affairs that are the least thing capable of independent existence. Perhaps in the rational sciences we should recognize similar necessities. I've already suggested that this is the case for the Entailment Principle itself.

Laws of logic and mathematics. We have discussed laws of nature. I suggest that we should postulate laws in logic and mathematics (non-contradiction, excluded middle in logic,

Peano's axioms for number, or whatever laws logicians and mathematics wish to postulate). In the light of the nature of proof just argued for we might suggest that such laws might be all we needed to postulate in the way of an ontology for logical and mathematical entities. These laws, if they are true laws, will be necessary rather than the contingent laws of nature (as I have argued the latter to be). One advantage of laws is that they assist in the project of instantiating (in space-time) all actually existing entities. For uninstantiated entities, laws can serve to explain the lure of the uninstantiated cases. They do this just as laws of nature serve, by acting as truthmakers for the counterfactuals having this form: if such and such entities had existed then they would have had such and such a nature. This, besides the economies it offers, promises to save us from having to postulate Platonic entities in addition to the empirical world!

As I have suggested already, there is the further question just what the truthmakers for these laws are. My present disposition is to see them as objective necessities in the world. But some more reductionist account may be tenable.

Chapter 13

Numbers

A metaphysics that aspires to a reasonable completeness must give an account of numbers. They are not the only mathematical entity, but they are central to mathematics and they are entities that philosophers have often discussed. Classes are nowadays thought to be fundamental to mathematics and so they also deserve discussion. I begin with numbers, starting with the natural numbers. My views on number evolved in discussions with Peter Forrest, and I used to think of it as the Forrest-Armstrong theory. We were later shown by John Bigelow that the same sort of theory was held by Isaac Newton. Still later there was the suggestion from James Franklin that we were close to Aristotle's account.

Suppose that there are seven black swans on the lake now. We want, you may be surprised to learn, a property and a mereological sum. The property in this case is a very second-rate sort of property: *black swan at present on the lake*. The mereological sum is the sum of these black swans. The property and the mereological sum are terms of a relation, and our claim was (and is) that the *relation* is an instantiation of the natural number 7. The property can be thought of as a 'cookie cutter' that cuts the mereological sum into just 7 black swans. (But notice that this neat division will not hold for every case. Consider two

delineated squares on a surface where they overlap and where the overlap is itself a small square. There are three delineated squares.) Notice that the relation is an internal one. It holds solely in virtue of the nature of its two terms: the property and the mereological whole of these swans in this case. A special feature of the natural numbers is that they have a link with *classes*. That is not surprising. Classes are classes of *ones* (their members) so they will have a natural number, though perhaps the number for some classes is an infinite one.

Notice that the number is instantiated. If you get to one of the infinities it may be that the number is so big that nothing can instantiate it. There remains the possibility of instantiation (there are no impossible numbers, I assume) and this is enough for mathematics, which, as I have argued, requires only the *possibility* of instantiation.

The rational and the real numbers can be captured in a similar way, and it is an advantage of this theory that it gives analyses of these three sorts of number that allows their resemblance to be captured, something that is not done by the Frege-Russell theory (for which see Russell's *Introduction to Mathematical Philosophy*, Chapter VII).

With the rationals and the reals we have only to shift to proportions. The cookie cutter is some fixed quantity – the unit – that 'measures' the thing to be measured. The unit might be a pound and what is measured, potatoes say, may be ½ a pound. This ½ relation instantiates one of the rational numbers. The unit might be the radius of some circle and the thing measured might be the area of the circle, πr^2, a real number that will be instantiated only if there are perfect circles in the world.

I now point out that all this was largely anticipated by Isaac Newton and Aristotle. Newton wrote:

> By *Number* we understand not so much a Multitude of Unities, as [i.e. 'but'] the abstracted ratio of any *Quantity*, to another Quantity of the same kind, which we take for Unity.   (*Universal Arithmetic*, 1769. Quoted in Bigelow and Pargetter, 1990, p.60.)

(A Multitude of Unities is, presumably, a many-membered class.)

Aristotle said:

> 'the one' means the measure of some plurality, and 'number' means a measured plurality and a plurality of measures . . . The measure must always be some identical thing predicable of all the things it measures, e.g. if the things are horses, the measure is 'horse' . . . (*Metaphysics* 1088a 4–9, trans. W.D. Ross)

So Forrest and I were just going back to a 'classical' conception of number. Following Aristotle, there have to be *things*, entities in the world, that are numbered. If there is no such thing to be numbered, perhaps because the number is too big, then the number is not instantiated and strictly it is only a possibility. This need not worry the mathematician, of course. 'Existence' for mathematics, I have argued, depends only on the possibility of instantiation. Provided there is a proof, the truthmakers for the axioms from which this proof starts, plus the Entailment Principle, will provide truthmakers for the possibility, and that is all that is needed.

We do need, though, to consider a little more closely what it is to say that a number or other mathematical entity 'is instantiated'. Suppose that a certain particular at a certain time is exactly nine kilos in mass. Are we to say that there is a universal 'nine' instantiated by this particular? That does not seem right. All we seem to need is the universal *being*

nine kilos in mass. The number 9 needs, as it were, to be fleshed out in a concrete existent. The pure mathematician has to abstract the number 9 in thought from the state of affairs. It cannot be instantiated on its own. That is a false abstraction.

Chapter 14

Classes

David Lewis in his monograph *Parts of Classes* (1991) pointed out something that seems very important for the ontology of classes. Many-membered classes, he argues, are no more than mereological sums of singletons (unit-classes) of their members:

{a, b, c, d, . . .} is identical with {a} + {b} + {c} + {d} . . .

where '+' is mereological addition. Given this, the relation of a class to any sub-class turns out to be mereological. This account of many-membered classes may look strange at first sight, but I think that it really gets to the bottom of the nature of many-membered classes. For are not such classes just collections of ones? (Multitudes of Unities, in Newton's inspired words, if they are his own.)

This led Lewis to consider the nature of singletons, unit-classes, which he expressed great puzzlement over, heading one section of his book 'Mysterious Singletons'. He found them so puzzling that eventually he proposed what he called a 'structuralist' account of them. He meant that they could be interpreted as being different sorts of entity in different contexts. He also insisted (rightly, I think) that we have to make a distinction between an entity and its singleton, between x and x's unit class, singleton {x}. (For his rather technical discussion see his Chapter 2: 'The Trouble with Classes'.)

I myself suggested in an article that the unit-classes, the singletons, are states of affairs (Armstrong 1991b). The thought was this. The unit-class marks off its member as a *one*, something that can be specified, put in a class. But don't you need some answer to the question 'What sort of one?' Ought there not to be some property, however second-rate the property, to single out the singular object? So what we have is some entity with some property, and that is a monadic state of affairs. This suggestion ran into trouble, though. Gideon Rosen showed that linking classes and states of affairs in this simple way ran into very serious trouble, including paradoxes (Rosen 1995).

I now think however that I got into this trouble by not drawing the same distinction for set theory that I draw in my discussion of mathematical truths. Let us turn to a particular case that I hope may prove enlightening. Consider the world, the whole of being, that at an earlier point I called w. w has the structural property W, the most extensive property of all. The all-embracing state of affairs is *w is W*, and states of affairs are particulars.

Suppose, then, that we propose that a unit-class exists of which *w is W* is the only member: $\{w$ is $W\}$. That is fine by a set theorist. There will also be singleton classes of this class, and so *ad infinitum*. But that is then trouble for the idea that all classes are states of affairs. This is because in a state of affairs, as I have developed the view, a property must attach to a particular *contingently*, not necessarily. But what property can attach *contingently* to *w is W*? Since w is everything, it embraces every actual property. So no contingent state of affairs is constructible! So I must deny existence to the singleton $\{w$ is $W\}$. I have to argue that we can't get further than the state of affairs that *w is W*. Anything more is a

mere possibility and we have seen that mere possibilities are no ontological addition to reality. So I realized that I should have said, at best, that *some* and only some classes are states of affairs. Metaphysics rules. Set theory (or any other logical or mathematical system) does not rule in ontology. Just because, given *w is W*, one can have set-theoretically {*w is W*} should not make us think that the singleton class {*w is W*} can be added to the *ontology*.

The situation is really the same as in, say, considering the infinity of the natural numbers. It may be that the world is not big enough to instantiate such an infinite number, much less the higher infinities. It is worth looking here at an interesting protest made by the US philosopher Nelson Goodman, friend and collaborator with Quine, about set theory.

In his book *The Structure of Appearance* (1966) he makes an impassioned plea about classes:

Thus when one uses and is unable to dispense with variables taking classes as values, *one cannot disclaim the ontological commitment.* [My italics] Use of the calculus of classes, once we have admitted any individuals at all, [for Goodman 'individuals' are what there is] opens the door to all classes, classes of classes, etc., of those individuals, and so may import . . . an infinite multitude of other entities that are not individuals. Supposedly innocent machinery may in this way be responsible for more of the ontology than are the special frankly [sic] 'empirical' primitives.   (p.35)

I share Goodman's indignation with *a priori* metaphysics. But what we should do about it, I think, is to treat set theory as if it were a branch of mathematics, and then think of these disciplines as concerned with *possibility*. Some mathematical structures, though, and this includes classes, may not be instantiated. Ontology should be restricted to the instantiated

classes. Furthermore, the members of these classes should exist. The class of the Greek gods, for instance, should not be admitted into our ontology.

One other thing that I think we should ban from our ontology is the null class, said by set theorists to be included in every class. Even the set theorists seem to agree that this is the part of their formalism that does not have to be taken with ontological seriousness. Where would you put the null class? Can space-time enfold it?

Chapter 15

Time

The last two chapters take up two issues that deserve ontological attention. The *Presentist* theory of time, and also the
Growing Block theory of time, take issue with the idea that
the whole of time exists. Truthmaker arguments are not
conclusive against these theories, but I think they make a
strong case. This is argued in this chapter. The last chapter is
about the mind. The mind is a remarkable phenomenon and
it can be argued with some plausibility that it is something
that my sort of metaphysics struggles with.

First we look at Presentism, the view that only the present
exists. The obvious problem for Presentism is that of finding
truthmakers for truths about the past or the future, which on
this theory do not exist. The problem is made even harder by
truths involving relations that hold between something that is
present and something that is past or future ('Five years ago,
I . . . ', 'Five minutes from now, I will . . .'). How can the
Presentist provide truthmakers for such truths? Only, it would
seem, by appealing to something in the present that has a
necessary connection to what came before, or is to come. But
what will these entities be? Whatever solution is found, either
by denying that such truths need truthmakers, or by postulating rather strange truthmakers, it would seem to be inferior to
the omnitemporal theorist's position that the past and the present both exist and stand in temporal relations to the present.

Can it be said by a Presentist that there *was* a past and there *will be* a future? But the bite of the argument from truthmakers is that there seems to exist no truthmakers for the Presentist to appeal to. Can the Presentist reply that there *were* truthmakers for the past, and *will be* truthmakers in the future? But what truthmakers can be given for these tensed truths? The Presentist will have to modify truthmaker theory, making what is present the only *existent* truthmakers. This seems to me a very artificial modification. Suppose that *a* produces present *b* although *a* lies in the past. The causal relation here has two terms, only one of which exists. Perhaps the Presentist will be prepared to accept this consequence, but it is surely unattractive.

That is not the only difficulty that faces the Presentist. Presentists are faced with the scientific theory of Special Relativity, now of great respectability, which relativizes the present, making it relative to the inertial frames of observers. Some philosophers and some scientists still defend the notion of a non-relative present, but it is clear that Presentism is open to objections from the standard cosmological view.

A third difficulty, which may be an original argument, asks how long the duration of the present is. Ordinary language behaves likes a concertina, expanding and contracting at will. One can say 'Now in the Christian era . . .' or we can say with Iago taunting Desdemona's father 'Now, now, very now, an old black ram is tupping your white ewe'. What will the Presentists say? In all consistency, must they not contract the metaphysical present? Won't they have to contract it at least to what psychologists used to call 'the specious present'? But even in momentary experience there is still a past and a present to be distinguished. Must not the Presentist contract the present to the least moment of

time? Anything more seems arbitrary. But that will make the present a theoretical entity which none of us can experience, an ironic position for a theory that presumably wants to base itself on experience – experience of the present.

I am not saying that there cannot be truthmakers that the Presentist can suggest. All I contend for is that implausible and complex truthmakers will have to be postulated instead of the straightforward truthmakers that the omnitemporal theorist can give.

Besides these arguments, we can also, I think, explain away the appeal of Presentism. For all non-human animals the present (the short-ranging present) is overwhelmingly the most *important* thing in their lives. And even for humans it is pretty central. If you don't get to do something right in the present – crossing a crowded road say – then maybe you won't get anything right later. Present impulses overwhelmingly take precedence over the counsels of prudence, which is why prudence is so difficult. 'Living in the present' is natural to us. This genuine biological importance to us of the short-term present then gets translated, I suggest, into bad philosophy.

The Growing Block theory[1] is the view that the past, right up to the present, is real, but agrees with Presentism that the future does not exist. It seems to me to be a much better theory than Presentism. It also has its romantic side. As it were, the existential quantifier (existence) sweeps forward, continually creating new being, with the present the edge beyond which there is nothing. The present is just the growing edge of being. The view still has to face the objection from Special Relativity that the present is not

---

[1] In *Truth and Truthmakers* I used the unlovely term 'pastism'.

absolute. Michael Tooley (1997) faces up to this point, and argues that it is possible to defend an absolute account of the present compatible with Special Relativity.

His problem, though, is the future. He uses the truthmaker argument as one argument for the continuing reality of the past. But he does not seem to be troubled about the allegedly non-existent future, against which we can again employ the truthmaker argument. A Growing Block theorist could try John Heil's way out by saying that there will be truthmakers in the future for truths about the future. But if present *a* produces the future effect *b*, only the first term of the relation exists while the second term does not yet exist, although it will exist. Not a very satisfactory view, I think.

Those who think the future does not exist are, I think, misled by the huge cognitive gap there is between the past and the future. 'What's to come is still unsure' (Shakespeare). But it exists for all that. This does not entail Fatalism. The will exists and acts causally, and to the extent that what is willed comes to be as a result of its being willed, we are free.

I end this chapter by quoting an authority, a very distinguished one. Albert Einstein wrote to a friend: 'The past, present and future are only illusions even if stubborn ones.' (Quoted by Paul Davies in an article 'The Mysterious Flow', p.25.)

Chapter 16

Mind

I finish this little sketch of an ontology by considering briefly the ontology of mind. As a physicalist I originally thought, when young, that Gilbert Ryle's *Concept of Mind*, read as a sophisticated behaviourism, might do the trick for the mind. I was always troubled, though, by the apparent denial of introspection. Ayer's clever remark that a behaviourist must pretend to be anaesthetized struck home. I gave up on the Rylean view after hearing Jack Smart read his later famous paper 'Sensations and Brain Processes' on a visit to Melbourne where I was a lecturer at the time. Smart himself graduated from a Rylean position under the influence of U.T. Place who, in his pioneering 1956 paper 'Is Consciousness a Brain Process?', had answered yes to this great question.

As I see it the identity of the mind with brain, an identity I would like to uphold, faces three separate problems: consciousness, *qualia*, and intentionality. I feel confident that consciousness can be dealt with without too much trouble, but *qualia* – such things as colour, sound, taste, and smell – together with the problem of *intentionality* are difficult. I am (surprising myself a little) less confident of my views on these two problems than I am of most of the arguments of earlier chapters of this book!

Before taking on these three topics, let me first address those who think that it is obviously wrong that the mind is

simply our brain at work, operating very probably according to exactly the same laws of nature that are operating in the rest of space-time. When, using our introspective powers, we turn our attention to our own minds we find nothing that suggests that the mental processes we are monitoring are processes in the brain. Indeed, I think that many would have held, up to quite recently, that introspective evidence shows, perhaps conclusively, that the mind is *not* the brain. We can call this the Argument from Introspection. The brain may be the immediate cause that sustains the mind in its operations, upholders of this argument often concede, but it is not the mind itself.

I believe that there is a simple observation that explains why the anti-materialist position should seem attractive even while it may be false. Unfortunately, I had not noticed the point when I published my book *A Materialist Theory of the Mind* (1968a), so I was not able to include it in the book. But I did publish a little article in *Analysis* in 1968: 'The Headless Woman Illusion and the Defence of Materialism'. This illusion is brought about by exhibiting a woman (or, of course, a man!) against a totally black background with the head of the woman swathed with the same black material. It is apparently very striking, and could lead unsophisticated persons to think that the woman lacks a head. It is clear what is going on here. The spectators cannot see the head, and as a result make a transition to a strong impression that there was no head to see. An illegitimate operator shift is at work, taking people from *not* seeing the head to seeming to see that the woman did *not* have a head. The shift of the 'not', the operator, occurs because it is, in the circumstances, the natural and *normally effective* way to reason. If you can't see anybody in the room, you may conclude, very reasonably, there is

nobody in the room. In general you will be right. In the same way, we emphatically do not perceive introspectively that the mind is material process in our heads, so we have the impression that it is *not* material. This seems to nullify the force of the Argument from Introspection, while still explaining the seductiveness of that reasoning.

Consciousness. There are various understandings of this word, but here I am concerned with our unmediated access to (some) of our own mental processes. We have here an access (which of course can be erroneous even if direct) which each of us has to our own mind. A demystifying thought here is that each of us has perceptual access to goings on in our own *body* that nobody except ourselves has. One such route of such access is proprioception: the sense of our orientation, including motion, of one's limbs in space. In the same way, though more thoroughly private, we have access to our own minds. In Locke and Kant this becomes a doctrine of 'inner sense'. The most striking parallel with sense perception is that just as ordinary perception gives us up-to-the-moment information about what is going on in our environment, so 'introspective awareness' gives us up-to-the-moment information as to (some of) what is going on in our minds at that time. We even get a doubling-up, we can be aware that we are aware.

By the way, I do not think that the privacy of our own thoughts and experiences is a logical privacy. The privacy is contingent. We know that there are Siamese twins who have some portion of their bodies in common. It seems a possibility, though it is not clear whether it is an empirical possibility, that there could be twins that have a portion of their brain in common, and further can both introspect some of the mental processes in this common portion.

What is the biological importance of introspective awareness for our public conduct of our lives? I think it is of
enormous importance for the solving of practical problems.
We need first to draw a distinction in the mental realm that
we readily draw in the bodily case. We easily distinguish
between *acts* of ours, such as raising our hand, perhaps to
vote, and our hand just going up, say because it gets entangled
with a rope that pulls our hand up whether we will or no. In
the first case, our will is active, in the second case something
unwilled happens to our arm. The same sort of distinction is
to be found in our mental life. Our thoughts can just drift
without, as it were, us doing anything conscious to control
the flow. But at other times we can be thinking, perhaps
aiming to achieve some purpose in the world. That is mental
action. (See Richard Taylor's *Action and Purpose*, 1966, for a
very clear and useful discussion.)

Now if anything is needed in the carrying out of an action,
at any rate any action that takes some time, it is *feedback*.
Consider crossing a busy road and how much visual and
other perceptual feedback is required to accomplish this. We
may infer, then, that when we do actively do something
in our mind, say adding up a column of figures, we are in
continual need of mental feedback. I suggest that this is the
biological reason we have introspective awareness. Without
it we could not solve problems 'in our heads'. Without
such feedback there could not be even the most primitive
culture, still less civilization. We may note that at least the
higher mammals – apes, elephants, the big cats – show signs,
at times, of solving practical problems 'in their heads'. So
perhaps they have some introspective capacities. The classic
case here is Kohler's chimpanzee that was introduced to boxes
to play with. At a certain point a banana was introduced too

high for the ape to get at on a single box. The chimp seemed puzzled, and sat down, apparently to think. Suddenly he acted, placed one box on another and found it easy to get the banana. One might speculate that an image came to him of one box on another and he recognized it as a solution to his problem (*The Mentality of Apes*, 1925).

Qualia. What Locke called secondary qualities, colour, sound, taste, smell, perhaps pain, itch, and so forth, notoriously pose a huge problem for scientific realism. They are clearly part of the manifest image of the world, as Wilfrid Sellars would have said. But can we accept them in the scientific image? We can accept light waves, sound waves, molecules that act on the taste and smell receptors, stimulation of pain receptors, and so on. There we can produce plausible enough theories. But part of what we started with, the secondary qualities, fits into the picture very badly.

The theory that I would like to uphold is that the secondary qualities are to be identified with the properties of objects as they begin to be revealed to us by the advance of scientific knowledge. Consider the blue surface of the mouse pad that I have beside my computer. It presents itself as a fairly uniform darkish blue surface with very small white specks in the pattern. I want to accept that the surface is for the most part blue. Perception presents us with the blueness as an objective property of something in the world and I think we should accept this, accept that the blue colour is in the world qualifying the pad. Science presents us with an apparently very different account involving light waves interacting with the fine structure of the physical surface of the pad reflecting light waves into my eyes. But I want to *identify* the colour surface with what the physicists tell us is going on there. It is a second identity theory alongside the identity of mental

processes with brain processes. (I first proposed this second identity theory in Chapter 12 of *A Materialist Theory of the Mind*, 1968a.)

If this identity is not accepted, then the ontological status of the secondary properties becomes very strange. They become at best properties that are *correlated* with certain physical goings on, as opposed to being identified with them. The laws involved fit in very badly with the structure of the other physical laws. They are, in a phrase that Jack Smart took from Herbert Feigl, *nomological danglers*. The laws that would be needed would dangle from the main structure of the physical laws in a thoroughly arbitrary and unprepossessing way. It is hard to believe that the world works this way. There are also difficulties that suggest that the secondary qualities are epiphenomenal, thus raising the problem about how we could know about their existence. The argument is that the following counterfactual proposition looks to be true: if these properties did not exist, the world would still work in the same way. The physical laws would ensure that our material brain would still work the same way, and so our experience would still be the same.

At the same time, the identity theory for the secondary qualities seems, as a matter of phenomenology, pretty incredible. All our experience seems to be contradicted when we are told that colour surfaces are really utterly different from what they appear to be. What we have in fact is light waves impacting upon a physical surface. The microstructure of the events that are going on are far too small to be captured by our vision. We are not aware of them. What is needed is some consideration that will make the suggested identity in some way plausible. We want an equivalent to the Headless Woman! I suggest that an Argument from Magnification may

help. We know that at a distance the detail of, say, some fine classical house, may not be apparent. The details merge to present something that is simpler in appearance. Only as we approach the house do the differences of parts of the structure appear. In much the same way we can get closer, as it were, to a uniformly coloured surface by looking at portions of it with a magnifying glass and then under successively more powerful microscopes. Our experience then is that more and more structure is revealed – it is no longer a uniform surface. We are handicapped in capturing the structure by the fact that human vision is only sensitive to light waves in a restricted band of the spectrum. But do we not have some evidence that what we are dealing with is microstructures quite unlike the surface presented to the eye in ordinary conditions? The rest of the secondary qualities are less precise than the qualities we are presented with in vision. But using the analogy of colour we can perhaps suppose that if there were equivalents of the magnifications that we can actually have in vision, then the other secondary qualities would break down in the same way that colour seems to do.

I am far from thinking my argument does anything to *prove* the identity of the secondary qualities with physically respectable properties. All I have wanted to do is to show how this identity can be given *some* epistemic respectability, *some* intuitive plausibility. The difficulty in fitting irreducible secondary qualities into our current physics in a plausible manner must be the main positive argument for reducibility. So I remain unimpressed by the case for irreducibility, for which, in our time, David Chalmers has so ably argued. See his book: *The Conscious Mind: In Search of a Fundamental Theory* (1996).

Intentionality. The last problem in the philosophy of mind that I will discuss is the intentionality of mental states. (The philosopher who first focused our attention on intentionality, using that word, was the Austrian Franz Brentano, 1838–1917. The English-speaking philosophical tradition was slow to come to terms with intentionality.) Certainly many mental states have this puzzling property, and for myself I incline to think that all mental states are intentional. (I have been influenced here, over many years, by the work of that leading philosopher of the mind, W.G. Lycan.) To possess intentionality, mental states must point to some object *but that object may not exist*. Beliefs are an obvious, non-controversial case because they may be false. In such a case, the 'thing believed' does not exist. A bit more controversially, I would argue that all perceptions are intentional. Of their own nature, they make a claim about reality, but the claim may be mistaken. Sensory illusion makes this clear, even when, using a more sophisticated part of our mind, we recognize that the presentations are illusions. This extends also, I think, to introspective claims. (Introspective claims don't have the indubitable nature that philosophers used to claim for them, perhaps influenced by Descartes.) In all these cases we have *informational* intentionality. But there is also intentionality present in intentions, purposes, desires (even if we are certain that the desired object is unattainable) and so on. The intentionality of mental states and processes is thus a very strange phenomenon. It is the mind somehow pointing out to the world (and including pointing inward to itself), but where it may be pointing wrong.

But if one is looking for a physicalist account of the mental, and so for a physicalist account of intentionality, I think we do well to notice the resemblance of intentionalities

to *dispositions*. I am not quite sure who first pointed this out, but I arrived at the idea on hearing a paper read by Dr John Burnheim many years ago in the Philosophy Department at Sydney University. Dispositions have *manifestations*. The brittle glass may manifest its disposition of brittleness by breaking rather easily. But, of course, it may never break, perhaps during its whole history. It might end by being melted down without breaking at any point. So manifestations of a disposition possessed by a certain object may or may not ever come into existence. That is why the fragile glass does not bear a *relation* to the manifestation. The manifestation may not occur, and the glass cannot be related to something that may never happen. But intentionality is like that too. If you have a false belief its content, say 'that it will rain today', may be perfectly clear. But you can't be *related* to that content because the belief is false. There is no rain. This suggests (without, of course, in any way proving) that intentionality may be some sort of cousin to dispositions, or even a peculiarly sophisticated disposition.

But how to develop this idea further is a problem! One presumably starts with simpler cases and then tries to work up. In my *A Materialist Theory of the Mind* I included a section in Chapter 11, not a very easy one, that I labelled 'The intentionality of perception'. The central idea, though, is not too difficult. I called it a *causal circuit*. Suppose that an organism is able to select between a certain range of colours. 'Select' here is behavioural. Suppose, that is, an object having one of the surface colours (blue, say) acts upon the organism that is then able to differentiate *in its conduct* (which could be 'conduct' within the mind, at least in the human case) between blueness and the other colours. Then it can be said to perceive blue *as blue*. That is primitive intentionality. All

this, of course, is routine in experiments to see whether organisms are capable of certain sensory discriminations. It is a *causal* circuit because the blue object acts causally on the subject that then has the capacity to act back in some way that differentiates the blue object from non-blue objects. Notice that the *closing* of the circuit need not occur. For instance, the organism may not be interested! (That is why experimenters include *rewards* for suitable discriminations.) All that is needed is the *capacity* for closing the circuit to occur (perhaps in suitable contexts). Notice also that the differentiation, if performed, can be seen as primitive *action*. Primitive intentionality is there in the action as much as in the perception.

That has not taken us very far. A sorting machine would be very near having that sort of intentionality. But I think we can see that complicating that sort of picture might begin to capture the intentionality of perception and even of action. But I can't see how to advance on this at all clearly. One can certainly agree with Saul Kripke that a causal chain from an object, event, etc. to the *naming* (or definite description?) of that object is going to be important, perhaps even essential, to it. But it is objects in our immediate environment, it would seem, that we ought to be considering first because that is what organisms can react to in the first place. The name 'Aristotle' (a case that Kripke called attention to) is harder because of the great distance in time. There is definitely a causal chain back to the great philosopher, but what else is there? Consider, again, the furthest reaches of intentionality, that is, the intentional objects of our most abstract and sophisticated utterances (including philosophical ones!), not to mention the plentiful supply of non-existent entities that we mention in our speech and our thoughts. I do not know

how to refute the claim that intentionality is an irreducible phenomenon, a phenomenon that is something different from the physical processes in the brain. So in my philosophy of mind I face difficulties from the alleged *qualia* and from the phenomenon of intentionality that seem rather greater than anything I am aware of in the rest of my ontological scheme.

Summing up. The following hypothesis has been argued for. The world is the space-time world. Its ultimate nature is a structure of contingent states of affairs (Russell's facts); and these states of affairs have as constituents particulars and universals, the latter monadic, dyadic, triadic, etc. with the details of this adicity determined empirically. The universals are linked (non-superveniently) by connections between states of affairs *types*. These constitute instantiations of the laws of nature. It seems necessary, further, to follow Russell again and recognize totality states of affairs that set limits to what there is, thus introducing negativity into the world, though I hope there is no need to accept absences, while providing truthmakers for truths that ostensibly refer to absences. Mathematical and logical and set-theoretical structures exist insofar as they are instantiated. If not, they are mere possibilities, and so (as I have argued) do not involve any addition of being.

References

Alexander, Samuel (1920). *Space, Time and Deity* (2 vols.). London: Macmillan.

Anderson, John (2007). *Space, Time and the Categories: Lectures on Metaphysics 1949–50*, ed. Creagh Cole. Sydney: Sydney University Press.

Aristotle (1941). *The Basic Works of Aristotle*, ed. Richard McKeon. New York: Random House.

Armstrong, D. M. (1968a). *A Materialist Theory of the Mind*. London: Routledge & Kegan Paul.

—— (1968b). 'The Headless Woman Illusion and the Defence of Materialism'. *Analysis*, 29, 48–9.

—— (1978a). *Nominalism and Realism*. Cambridge: Cambridge University Press.

—— (1978b). *A Theory of Universals*. Cambridge: Cambridge University Press.

—— (1983). *What is a Law of Nature?* Cambridge: Cambridge University Press.

—— (1989). *Universals: An Opinionated Introduction*. Boulder, Colorado: Westview Press.

—— (1991a). 'What Makes Induction Rational?'. *Dialogue* (Canada), 30, 503–11.

—— (1991b). 'Classes are States of Affairs'. *Mind*. 100, 189–200.

—— (1995). 'Reply to Rosen'. *Australasian Journal of Philosophy*, 73, 626–8.

—— (1997a). *A World of States of Affairs*. Cambridge: Cambridge University Press.

—— (1997b). 'Against Ostrich Nominalism: A Reply to Michael Devitt'. In *Properties*, eds. D.H. Mellor and Alex Oliver, Oxford: Oxford University Press.

Armstrong, D. M. (1999). *The Mind-Body Problem: An Opinionated Introduction*. Boulder, Colorado: Westview Press.

—— (2004a). *Truth and Truthmakers*. Cambridge: Cambridge University Press.

—— (2004b). 'Going through the Open Door Again: Counterfactual versus Singularist Theories of Causation'. In *Causation and Counterfactuals*, eds. John Collins, Ned Hall, and L.A. Paul, Cambridge, Mass.: MIT Press.

Ayer, A.J. (1947). *Language, Truth and Logic*. London: Victor Gollancz.

Bigelow, John and Pargetter, Robert (1990). *Science and Necessity*. Cambridge: Cambridge University Press.

Black, Max (1952). 'The Identity of Indiscernibles'. *Mind*, 61, 152–64. Reprinted with some additions in his *Problems of Analysis: Philosophical Essays*, London: Routledge & Kegan Paul, 1954.

Black, Robert (2000). 'Against Quidditism'. *Australasian Journal of Philosophy*, 78, 87–104.

Bradley, F.H. ([1893] 1946). *Appearance and Reality*. Oxford: Clarendon Press.

Butler, Joseph ([1736] 1906). *The Analogy of Religion*. London: J.M. Dent (Everyman's Library).

Chalmers, David J. (1996). *The Conscious Mind: In Search of a Fundamental Theory*. Oxford: Oxford University Press.

Davies, Paul (2002). 'That Mysterious Flow'. *Scientific American*, 287, Sept. special issue, 24–9.

Devitt, Michael (1997). ' "Ostrich Nominalism" or "Mirage Realism"?' In *Properties*, eds. D.H. Mellor and Alex Oliver, Oxford: Oxford University Press.

Dowe, Phil (2000). *Physical Causation*. Cambridge, Cambridge University Press.

Dretske, F.I. (1977). 'Laws of Nature'. *Philosophy of Science*, 44, 248–68.

Ellis, Brian (2001). *Scientific Essentialism*. Cambridge: Cambridge University Press.

Gigerenzer, Gerd (2002). *Reckoning with Risk*. London: Penguin Books.

Goodman, Nelson (1966). *The Structure of Appearance*. Indianapolis: Bobbs-Merill.

Harman, G. (1965). 'The Inference to the Best Explanation'. *Philosophical Review*, 74, 88–95.

Horwich, Paul (1990). *Truth*. Oxford: Basil Blackwell.

Hume, David (1960). *A Treatise of Human Nature* ed. L.A. Selby-Bigge. Oxford: Clarendon Press.

Jackson, Frank (1977). 'Statements about Universals'. In *Properties*, eds. D.H. Mellor and Alex Oliver, Oxford: Oxford University Press.

Johnson, W.E. (1921 & 1924). *Logic*, vol. 1 (1921) & vol. 3 (1924). New York: Dover.

Kennedy, Brian (1995). *A Passion to Oppose*. Melbourne: Melbourne University Press.

Kohler, Wolfgang (1925). *The Mentality of Apes*. London: Kegan Paul, Trench, Trubner & Co.

Lewis, David (1991). *Parts of Classes*. Oxford: Basil Blackwell.

—— (1999). 'New Work for a Theory of Universals'. Chapter 1 in *Papers in Metaphysics and Epistemology*, by David Lewis, Cambridge: Cambridge University Press.

Lipton, Peter (2004). *Inference to the Best Explanation*. London and New York: Routledge.

MacBride, Fraser (2005). 'The Particular-Universal Distinction: A Dogma of Metaphysics'. *Mind*, 114, 565–614.

Martin, C.B. (2008). *The Mind in Nature*. Oxford: Oxford University Press.

Molnar, George (2000). 'Truthmakers for Negative Truths'. *Australasian Journal of Philosophy*, 78, 72–86.

—— (2003). *Powers*, ed. Stephen Mumford. Oxford: Oxford University Press.

Mulligan, Kevin, Simons, Peter, and Smith, Barry (1984). 'Truthmakers'. *Philosophy and Phenomenological Research*, 44, 287–321.

Mumford, Stephen (2007). *David Armstrong*. UK: Acumen.

Newstead, Anne and Franklin, James (forthcoming). 'On What Exists Mathematically: Indispensability without Platonism'.

Oddie, Graham (1982). 'Armstrong on the Eleatic Principle and Abstract Entities'. *Philosophical Studies*, 41, 285–95.

Pap, Arthur (1959). 'Nominalism, Empiricism and Universals: I'. *Philosophical Quarterly*, 9, 330–40.

Place, U.T. (1956). 'Is Consciousness a Brain Process?'. *British Journal of Psychology*, 47, 44–50.

Quine, W.V. (1961). *From a Logical Point of View*. New York: Harper & Row.

Ramsey, F.P. ([1925] 1997). 'Universals'. In *Properties*, eds. D.H. Mellor and Alex Oliver, Oxford: Oxford University Press.

——([1927] 1990). 'Facts and Propositions'. In *Philosophical Papers*, ed. D. H. Mellor, Cambridge: Cambridge University Press.

Restall, Greg (1995). 'What Truthmakers Can Do for You'. Canberra: Automated Reasoning Project, Australian National University.

Rodriguez-Pereyra, Gonzalo (2002). *Resemblance Nominalism: A Solution to the Problem of Universals*. Oxford: Oxford University Press.

Rosen, Gideon (1995). 'Armstrong on Classes as States of Affairs'. *Australasian Journal of Philosophy*, 73, 613–25.

Russell, Bertrand ([1910–11] 1949). 'Knowledge by Acquaintance and Knowledge by Description'. Reprinted in *Mysticism and Logic*, London: Allen & Unwin.

——([1918] 1972). *The Philosophy of Logical Atomism*. Reprinted in *Russell's Logical Atomism,* ed. David Pears, London: Fontana Books.

——(1920). *Introduction to Mathematical Philosophy*. London: Allen & Unwin.

——(1948). *Human Knowledge: Its Scope and Limits*. London: Allen & Unwin.

Ryle, Gilbert (1949). *The Concept of Mind*. London: Hutchinson.

Sachs, Oliver (1986). *The Man Who Mistook His Wife for a Hat*. London: Picador Books.

Searle, John R. (1969). *Speech Acts*. Cambridge: Cambridge University Press.

Sellars, Wilfrid (1968). *Science and Metaphysics*. London: Routledge & Kegan Paul.

Shoemaker, Sydney (1984). *Identity, Cause, and Mind*. Cambridge: Cambridge University Press.

Taylor, Richard (1966). *Action and Purpose*. New Jersey: Prentice Hall.

Tooley, Michael (1977). 'The Nature of Laws'. *Canadian Journal of Philosophy*, 7, 667–98.

—— (1997). *Time, Tense and Causation*. Oxford: Clarendon Press.

Van Fraassen, Bas C. (1987). 'Armstrong on Laws and Probabilities'. *Australasian Journal of Philosophy*, 65, 243–60.

Williams, Donald C. (1966). 'The Elements of Being'. In *Principles of Empirical Realism*, by D.C. Williams, Illinois: Charles C. Thomas.

Wilson, John Cook (1926). *Statement and Inference*, 2 vols. Oxford: Clarendon Press.

Wittgenstein, Ludwig (1922). *Tractatus Logico-Philosophicus*. Reprinted with a new translation by D.F. Pears and B.F. McGuinness, London: Routledge & Kegan Paul, 1961.

—— (1953). *Philosophical Investigations*. Trans. G.E.M. Anscombe. Oxford: Basil Blackwell.

Index

Lightning Source UK Ltd.
Milton Keynes UK
UKOW040735220612

194848UK00002B/2/P

ALSO BY STEFAN ZWEIG

Letter from an Unknown Woman

LETTER FROM AN UNKNOWN WOMAN is Stefan
Zweig's most terrifying rendition of a life brought
to its tragic conclusion by the unmitigated pursuit
of relentless desire. This is the story of unrequited
love of a woman for a man whose child she will
bear but who cares so little for her that he fails to
recognise her as she obsessively and painfully
pursues him. This extraordinary novella of dis-
torted passion and extreme behavior is one of
the most powerful modern renditions of the
strength and madness of love.

Also included in this volume is *The Fowler Snared*
which provides a cadenza to the theme, but in
this case it is the man who remains unknown and
whose passion is unrequited.

Max Ophuls's classic film, based on *Letter from
an Unknown Woman* appeared in 1948 starring
Louis Jourdan and Joan Fontaine.

ISBN 1 901285 05 7 · *92 pages* · £7

STEFAN ZWEIG

Beware of Pity

BEWARE OF PITY is a powerful novel which explores the complex hidden recesses of emotion. In 1913 a young second lieutenant discovers the terrible dangers of pity and eventually flees from them into the battlefield. His involvement begins with a *faux pas:* he had no idea the girl was lame when he asked her to dance. Paying her an occasional afternoon call seemed to give him a new sense of purpose and he did not notice how imperceptibly bound up with tenderness his concern might be. The girl's face brightened, her father doted, the young man's self-esteem rose. But he was gradually to learn that pity, like morphia, is only at first a solace to the invalid and unless one knows the exact dosage, and when to stop, it can become a virulent poison.

Beware of Pity is Stefan Zweig's only novel and is a devastatingly unindulgent realisation of the torment of betrayal of both honour and love, set against the background of the disintegration of the Austro-Hungarian Empire.

ISBN 1 901285 43 X · *474 pages* · £10